An Echo Through the Trees

By Michael Galloway

ISBN-13: 978-0-9847402-0-8

www.michaelgalloway.net

This is a work of fiction. Names, characters, places, and events are products of the author's imagination or are used fictitiously. Any resemblance to actual persons, living or dead, locations or events is entirely coincidental.

Chapter One

He popped open the tiny brown steel mailbox, but inside it was empty. Out of the rows and rows of dorm mailboxes, his began to feel like the emptiest of all. He turned away and hiked back upstairs to his room, pensive at each turn of the staircase, and outlined his next letter in his head.

After unlocking his third floor dorm room door, Chase Krause stepped inside to his own cherished world he called home. He brought in a massive carpet remnant at the beginning of the year, and although it slid around sometimes, anything was better than the icy tiled floor. Barren walls frustrated him, so he plastered them with posters of places he knew he would never travel to but admired anyway— Sydney, the Caribbean, and London. All of them made the room seem a bit crowded, but lived in.

He sat down into a school-provided, creaking, wooden chair and withdrew a pen and paper from inside his desk. He began to write:

Dear Dad,

I am now beginning my third month here at school. I'm still planning on being an architect, but like everyone else here, I have to get through prerequisites first.

You know, it's amazing how big this school really is. There are a lot of people here who really don't know what they want to do with themselves even after they have been here a few years. For some reason that always shocked me.

Mom is doing well, as usual. She seems to be taking my absence around the house pretty well these days. I still visit on weekends, though. But I am going hunting this weekend, and I know she'll miss me. It will be my second time hunting, and I wish you could be there. Maybe this time I can get a deer instead of having to tell the guys that the only bullet I used was the one that fell out of the tree stand. Ha, ha.

Sorry to keep this note short, but I have to get going. Going to practice at the rifle range this afternoon with Josh. Talk to you later,

Love,
Chase

P.S. Are you going to stop by for Christmas?

And so it ended. He paused a moment to survey his hands and the dusty desk before him. His hands were distinctly his father's— slender, strong, nimble—but nineteen. He knew his eyes were his mother's ocean blue, as was his blonde hair that was cut close on the sides.

He set his pen down, and creased the letter in two places. After withdrawing an envelope from inside of his desk, he slid the letter inside. He stamped it, sealed it, and then wrote on a return address. Then he wrote down the destination, but he was never sure if it was right because there had not been a response from there in years.

But that was no matter. He got up and slipped on his forest green winter jacket and matching gloves, and hoisting up his bags and black suitcase he turned to the door. He knew his friend, Josh, would be downstairs in the lobby any time now to pick him up for target practice. Chase stared at the letter a minute, then tucked it into his inside jacket pocket and opened the door.

He bounded back down the stairs and walked into the lobby. To his right was a lounge ringed with plush mauve chairs and a fireplace in the middle of the back wall. He turned to his left, back near the computer lab and the mailboxes and set down his suitcase and bags. To the right of the mailboxes was the office, where a resident could pick up their newspaper subscriptions, borrow a vacuum or trade their identification card for a basketball.

Beneath the ledge of office service window was the mail slot, and Chase kneeled down now to reach it. He turned away as he let his letter slide in, listening for the familiar clunk of the envelope hitting the bottom of the wastebasket that impersonated a mailbox. He felt like he was sending off yet another traveler, which would pass along with the rest of the mail like a caravan across the desert to his father, who, last he heard, lived in Reno, Nevada.

Chase picked up his luggage.

"Ready?" Josh piped.

"Yes. So who is going this time?"

"My uncle and my dad and us. Are we dropping your stuff off first?"

"Yeah. I said I'd stop by my Mom's tonight before we go. So it finally happened, huh? I mean, with Kelly?"

"What? Oh, her. She probably found somebody new. You know how it goes. Break up one day, new life the next." Josh's voice smacked of sarcasm.

"You're over her that fast?"

"Have to be," he replied, moving his mouth like he wanted to spit. "Oh, and don't say her name anymore. I've designated it a swear word."

Chase smirked and followed as Josh headed out to his car in the tiny, choked parking lot out in front of the dorm. To a passerby, the lot looked as if it only provided enough room when students were on vacation.

"So does your dad have all the stuff packed?" Chase asked.

"As always. But this time Uncle Jim is going to cart most of it up there."

"Is that safe?"

"You know how my Dad is about drinking and hunting. Dad told him not to bring any bottles up north. But I suppose he could always hit a bar on the way up. I didn't think of that."

Chase knew Neal Weldon, Josh's father, had the physical edge over his younger brother Jim. Although Neal had taken over the construction company where he worked, years of site labor molded his forearms into steel pistons.

"I'd hate to see something bad happen. It's been so long since I've been hunting," Chase said.

5

"Don't fret. Dad'll pull over if he sees anything."

"And what? Pound him?"

"No, he still has to be able to drive his own truck. That wouldn't be good."

"So did you bring a football?"

"Sure did. It's in the backseat. But I hope the hunt doesn't get that dull."

"Dull? I scored two touchdowns against you last time, Mack."

"You won't this time, Chevy," Josh countered.

"And why is that? You couldn't stop me before."

"Because this time we'll be on the same team."

Chase remembered how they both played neighborhood football back before college, and how Josh had enough girth to earn the nickname 'Mack'. At the time, when he ran the football at you, it felt like you had been hit by a mining truck. Chase earned the nickname 'Chevy', not like the actor, but rather the truck. Josh stood six feet tall, with brown hair and eyes like his father, but had an olive complexion like his mother's.

Chase dictated directions with his forefinger, as if Josh forgot. Josh turned down the curve which led to Chase's home in Richfield, a suburb on the fringes of South Minneapolis. Chase had lived with his mother, Karen, up until the start of college. They had stayed in the same house for years after the divorce and were fortunate enough to have had the majority of the mortgage paid off before the legal details were completely settled. Karen battled to keep the house in order while raising her only son, yet held on to her teaching position at the nearby elementary school.

Chase jumped out and opened the front door of the house. Stepping inside he noticed for the first time that the housework was being let go in places—a sweater over a chair, dishes stacked in the sink over there. He frowned and walked into his bedroom, stepping over a clump of clothes in the hallway.

To his left, a new painting hung on the hallway wall. Amazed and curious, he put his hand on the painting, letting its bumps and creases slide underneath his fingertips. It was an outdoor scene, with a grove of trees displaying their fall colors—crimsons, oranges and goldenrod yellows—huddled together, yet eager to explode. Could it be his mother's work? She had the potential, but she always painted portraits as far as he could remember.

Turning into his room, the bags and his suitcase came to rest next to his bed. On the highest shelf of the closet lay his Winchester 32 special, and next to it, a box of shells. Through constant coaxing Karen finally gave in to letting him keep the rifle in the house, so long as it never was loaded unless it was an emergency. Although there had never been a break-in at their house, his Mom often repeated the story about her childhood home being robbed once.

Chase returned to the living room and smiled as he passed by his Mom's easel and paints, where a half-finished painting of the season's first snow trapped his attention. In all the years he had seen her paint, he had never seen her paint this well. He could not believe she had it in her. *Maybe the state of the housework wasn't that important after all*, he thought.

A hasty note was left on the kitchen table next to the door as Chase returned to Josh's idling car. The engine revved as he opened the passenger door, and he slung his rifle case into the backseat.

"What?" Josh said, puzzled by Chase's sly smile.

"It's my Mom. She's painting again. I think I want to stop by the mall on the way back."

Josh turned to look over his shoulder and backed the car out of the driveway. "For what? Paints?"

"No, for a sale flyer. I heard there is going to be a sale this weekend in the mall for paintings. Maybe she could sell one. Who knows?"

Josh nodded and sped towards the highway which passed near the shooting range. Chase meanwhile calculated a plan in his mind, and although he did not believe it was right to tell his mother what to do, he did not think a little encouragement ever hurt. Presently, he opened up his box of shells. He counted one bullet missing, but he hoped this weekend he could bury that embarrassment forever.

Chapter Two

Karen Krause slung her petite purse onto the kitchen table, creating a whiff that sent a note cartwheeling onto the floor. She picked it up and squinted at its message:

Mom,

Went shooting at the range with Josh. Going hunting this weekend, but I'll be home around five for dinner. Talk to you later.

Love,
Chase

She held the note an extra minute before setting it back onto the table. Dinner would have to be started now if Chase were going to make it up north in time for the morning deer opener, she reasoned. She pulled pans out of the cupboard and began to mentally ready herself for her own private empty house.

The house had always been a difficult battle economically, and each element had been set in place—piece by excruciating piece. A full-time elementary teaching job did pay the bills, of course, and helped her to hang on to two out of three loves left in her life—her son and teaching.

After setting up dinner, she meandered over to the broom closet and withdrew a brown paper grocery bag and promptly began to stuff it with snacks. She slipped into Chase's bedroom and put it next to his suitcase, curling the top of the bag down, hoping he would assume it was a part of his things. Looking around, she was reminded of the precise order of his bedroom: the neatly pleated blue bedspread, the dusty airplane models perched atop his dresser, and the few stacked and ordered clothes inside the dresser itself. Suddenly, the clothes on the floor in the hallway embarrassed her and picking them up she put them into a clothesbasket.

Back in the living room, though, was a painting in need of completion. A jerk of a lamp chain illuminated a plush sofa, a large television, a bookshelf bulging with fiction, and her weathered easel. One look at the caked outsides of the jars of paint resting next to the easel aggravated that itch to get back to work.

She slipped on a white smock and proceeded to unscrew the paint jars. Hunching over her work, she reached down for her wooden palette and eyed the trees.

The painting depicted the end of fall, with muddied grass ceding to streaking snowflakes that resembled slow-motion raindrops. And then there were the trees—complicated black and brown networks absent of visible life.

In an effort to beat back the silence of the afternoon and of the coming night Karen pulled a chair up to the easel and promptly began stirring the paints. She was sure she could slip in an hour's worth of painting before dinner. She squeezed out some titanium white onto her palette and picked out a fine bristled brush.

She had stopped rendering people three paintings ago, and why she did not know. For some reason, the impulse had hit her a week after Chase left for college. The tap, tap, tapping sound of the bristles on canvas mimicked the current tapping of flakes occurring outside on the living room window. *But the trees—yes, the trees, they needed something.* Spreading more paint onto her palette, she decided to alter the desolation of the landscape.

Dotting in stray leaves whirling to the ground, she stumbled upon a possible secret purpose of the ritual of falling leaves. It was as if the purpose was to welcome the snow, leaving barren branches to capture it. In capturing the snow, though, a new beauty was released from within.

Satisfied at her progress, she leaned back now. The trees regained their life and instead of being dead brown things jutting out of the ground, they looked as if they were reaching.

Chapter Three

"Line is hot," said the man in charge of watching the shooters on the outdoor rifle range. With a jet-black crew cut and a complexion as smooth as the barrel of a rifle he strode back to his predictable stance ten feet behind the line. He puffed and chugged on the cigar stub jutting out of the corner of his mouth and stuffed his hands back into his jacket pockets, comfortable with boredom.

Chase cradled his rifle, its barrel resting on a sandbag for support. There were five stacks of sandbags in all, each pile resting five feet apart from each other on top of a long, chipped white wooden table. Each space remained occupied and as each shooter pulled off their shots, sending gunshot echoes hammering off their ear protectors. Chase fired his Winchester, temporarily forgetting about the recoil, until his numb shoulder reminded him. Josh lined up for his shot at the paper bull's eye clothespinned to a chicken-wire fence across the field.

"So she left you, huh?" Chase opened, oblivious to Josh's ear protectors.

Josh pulled the trigger. "What?" He replied, slipping off the headgear.

"I said, why did she leave you?"

"Didn't say. She didn't answer my phone calls. Nothing."

"A long distance relationship like that's gotta be tough."

"It is. I trusted her, but all we've done in the last couple of weeks is argue, mostly over little things...who I choose to talk to on campus, what time I call, you name it."

"Those are the things that kill you every time."

"All safeties on?" It was the line watcher again. He stepped up and scanned down the line for verbal confirmations. "Okay, go ahead," he nodded, as the five shooters trudged across the muddied field towards the targets that flapped in the wind.

"You're an expert on relationships, right?" Josh asked.

"Not really."

"C'mon. You've always given out good advice."

Chase rolled his eyes and clenched his lips. "You know I hate giving out advice on short notice. I didn't even know her that well."

"I'm thinking of calling her. You know sitting down at a restaurant when she comes back to town. To talk things out."

Chase stopped walking and turned to stop Josh with his hand.

"Josh, she's gone. You even acted like she was history back in the dorm. Get on with your life."

Josh rolled his eyes and paced up to the target. "That's cold. You're starting to sound like my Dad." He clipped on his target tighter, apparently admiring his near bull's-eye marksmanship.

Chase cringed. "Hey, you're in college now, right? If you can't meet a new one, you're doomed to extinction."

"I was just joking about the dad part. I didn't mean it that way. Honest. No, you're right." Josh pointed to Chase's target. "Decent shot, by the way. Only an inch off center."

As Chase smiled in appreciation. "Thanks."

The two marched back to the line, as Chase imagined their upcoming trip up north. For Chase, it would be the second hunting trip in his life since the first venture with Josh two years ago. He did not fell a deer, but it was no matter. The awe of a pink-tinged sky in the morning and the unbelievable sounds like the cracking of the trees in the wind or the barely audible tapping sound of snow falling off the branches made each minute of tedious packing worthwhile.

He knew Josh hoped to string together a third year of success, rivaling his father's younger days. Although Josh tried to explain his technique to the others, nobody could put a price on built-in budding intuition.

"So how's your mom been?" Josh broke in.

"I can't tell anymore. She seems happy, but she's letting the house go. There are clothes lying around all over, dishes left undone—it's like the little things are falling out of place."

"My Dad was like that with dirty socks until Mom starting throwing his clean ones on the floor, too."

Chase smirked, then straightened his features. "No, no. It's more than that. She's usually so precise about the house. At least her paintings are still precise. And those—she's painting new things, too. Outdoor scenes, now."

"She could sure do portraits good, that was for sure."

The two students reacquired their guns. The other three marksmen returned to the line and the line watcher gave his familiar signal. Over the next half-hour, the shots Chase fired were grouped tight near the bull's-eye.

Satisfied, both men collected their spent shells and their guns and headed in towards the gun shop at the edge of the range. A warm November wind greeted them as they marched in like kid soldiers readied for a war.

Inside the gun shop was a makeshift restaurant complete with long, shaky folding tables that reminded Chase of a church bingo hall. The odor of stale coffee lingered to complement the brown blotchy water stains covering a quarter of the ceiling. The countertops looked clean, but Chase wondered if the place had ever been swept. And although there were cracks in the walls that would make any architect shudder, Chase was humored to see someone at least made an attempt to paint over them.

Josh stared at the menu board, then the counter, and finally the cashier. Chase pondered the National Rifle Association posters encircling the room, most of which touted second amendment rights. A pair of hunters in their forties dressed in olive green camouflage jackets reclined at one of the tables. Both discussed the latest in high technology navigation devices, laughing over their cigarettes and coffee.

"What ken I get you boys? A sodee pop?" Piped the man behind the counter. His hair was an ashen gray, slicked back from his high forehead, and his barrel chest alone dwarfed the cash register. Chase could not place the accent, although it did seem from out of state. It wore on his nerves like dragging his fingers across a cheese grater, however.

"Yes, uh, two orange sodas please," Josh replied.

"A dollar for two," the man replied, taking Josh's money and turning to insert the bill into the vending machine behind him. With thick fingers, the cashier plugged the bill into the machine and out clunked a can of soda and two quarters. He then inserted the quarters for another can. Chase let the tension uncoil from his taut shoulders as the pop hit the counter. *Thank goodness, it was time to go*, he thought.

Josh lingered a moment to examine the glass case full of scopes and rifle accessories, but most of the equipment soared out of his price range. He turned away and as the two left, the stench of coffee haunted and harassed their senses, as did the boastful conversations of the two hunters. Their high price discussion reminded Chase of a time when Josh's father Neal tried to keep pace talking with a trio of hunters sitting at the same table. Neal floundered trying to discuss the latest navigational aids for deep woods hiking. That is, until Josh made up a story about getting going to the grocery store.

"Does he have to call us 'boys' like that? We are out of high school now," Chase said, wincing as they walked back to Josh's car.

"Oh, him? Don't let him get to you. He couldn't navigate his way out of his own backyard I bet."

Chase let out a snort of laughter and reclined back in the passenger seat. Josh started the car and drove on towards the shopping mall.

Meanwhile, Chase lowered his head slightly and stared at the dashboard. *What was it about the clerk that bothered me*, he thought. *Was it his looks, or was it his style? Maybe it was just the stink of the place.*

He fastened his safety belt. *No, it was the voice. The word "boys" specifically. Yes, the way he said "boys." It sounded like Dad.*

Lifting his eyes and shifting his gaze to the trees passing by outside the passenger window, he mused about the apparent deadness of their branches. But it was an illusion, of course, and to him the branches looked now as if they were reaching.

Chapter Four

Karen squeezed out the last drops of water from her paintbrushes when Chase came in through the kitchen door. He clutched a neon green flyer in one hand and the strap of the rifle case in the other. With a clunk the brushes dropped into the sink, as if in shame.

"Hi, Mom. I see you got my note. Here, I brought this for you," he thrust the flyer out with his right hand.

Puzzled, she approached and grabbed the paper. She read it aloud.

"Artist sale. This Saturday at the Maple Ridge Mall. Open 10 AM to 5 PM. Local artists can exhibit and sell their work. Donations to the local foodshelf welcome." She smiled politely, and set the flyer onto the kitchen table. Chase looked on, appearing to be disappointed by her lack of expression.

Then, in a burst of appreciation, she threw open her arms and wrapped them around him. "Thank you. That was very thoughtful of you."

She pulled back, holding her palms on his shoulders. "But I don't know if my paintings are good enough. It's just something I do on the side. A hobby. I never really thought about making money from it." The longer she dwelled on the whole thought of it, the more unsure she became. She crossed her arms and looked down at the table, but not at the flyer.

"C'mon. Give it a shot. What do you have to lose? Artists always say they're not good enough right before they make it big." Chase slipped the rifle case off of his shoulder and turned towards the hallway. Then, he sighed. "It's up to you. But I think you are more than good enough."

"Thanks," she replied again. Chase nodded and began to leave, but she turned to catch him. "By the way, Neal called and said not to forget to bring your socks. The wool and the cotton ones, I mean."

Chase nodded again and left for his bedroom. Karen turned her attention back to fixing dinner as the neglected baked beans on the stove began to bubble into a strange looking dome. It hurt her deeply to think how Chase's father used to make promises of taking his son hunting someday. Breaking a promise between two adults was one thing. Breaking one to your own son was the one thing she figured would gnaw away at even the most granite of hearts.

She spun around now to drain the water from the boiling potatoes. She recalled how Chase used to love showing off snapshots of his father, even after he had left. To her, though, Kenneth had transformed into a stranger overnight, and even their final meeting before the divorce court date ten years ago seemed awkward and forced. Unbearable blanks of silence separated them as they shared a final cup of coffee at a roadside diner he frequented as a trucker. All the time he babbled apologies, she alternately fumed and missed the brush of his hand on her cheek, thinking her competition was watching from some other table.

After setting the pan back onto the stove, she flipped up a loose coil of her blonde hair and began to twist and punch the masher into the potatoes. *Maybe, just maybe*, she thought, *he would stop by for Christmas this time around.* Then again, she remembered how the man stopped answering his phone years earlier it seemed, and the last Christmas present was sent six years ago and two weeks late.

There was one particular picture that hurt her most, however. It showed Chase sitting on the running board of his father's semi truck, with Kenneth standing next to him. Kenneth used to let Chase climb into the cab of the rig that he drove cross-country. It was a shining chrome dream playground for a ten-year-old boy. "Someday, I'll take you on a trip," his voice replayed in her mind. "One of these weekends."

She stabbed the serving fork into the middle of the Polish sausage in the skillet. Dinner was done.

Chase reappeared, dressed in a navy blue sweatshirt and matching sweatpants. "Need any help?" He offered.

"No, it's all ready," she said with an awkward smile. "Go on. Sit down."

She approached the table, cradling the pan of baked beans with tattered lime green potholders, and set it onto a heating pad. Chase reclined in one of the chairs and rested his wrists on the glass-topped table. She set down two forks and sat down across the table from him.

"So how is school?" She asked, in a quiet voice with no hint of feeling.

"Good."

"Do you like your teachers?" It was a natural curiosity for her, but it seemed awkward having said it now.

"So far. Except for the one professor with the monotone voice. Classes are bigger than I thought they would be, too, but I'm used to it now." Chase swirled his fork into his potatoes, distracted.

"Mom, what's it like to be in love?"

"You should know. You dated what's-her-name...Marie...for four months."

"She was a phony, ma."

"Oh. Well, then do you mean falling in love or being in love?"

"Being in love."

"I guess true love should make you feel like you can do anything. It's a kind of a completeness, a wholeness to your life. An invincibility, even."

"And when it's over?"

"Sometimes you think it was all a dream."

Karen looked down at her plate.

"Why do you ask?" She said after a moment.

"I think I ticked Josh off."

"Why?"

"I mean about his breakup with Kelly. I told him to get on with his life."

"I wish I could have heard that a few times. How's he taking it?"

"Okay, so far, which is weird."

"Maybe he is listening to your advice."

"Just as long as he doesn't shoot anybody on the trip."

Karen's eyes widened.

"I'm kidding, ma. I'm kidding."

A two-minute gulf of silence opened up between them, stretching the length of the table. Karen then broke the silence by getting up and rinsing her plate off in the sink. She then wedged her plate and fork into the dishwasher. Suddenly, she did not like the unfamiliar cluttered look of the house and started scrubbing the stove.

"Do you still write to your Dad?"

"Yeah." Chase got up from the table and set his plate into the sink, rinsing it. "I wrote him today. Should get there Monday or Tuesday. He'll write back, I know it." He then looked down at the floor for a moment.

"I'm sure he'll write back sometime," she replied, scrubbing furiously on the stovetop, careful to keep her head bowed and her frown out of sight.

Chase leaned his back against the sink, with his arms crossed. "So are you going to see Steve this weekend?"

"I might. I mean, I don't know. He seems, well, you know, too stuck-up for me. Other times he throws temper tantrums when he doesn't get his way. For having raised a kid on his own, he can sure act like one sometimes. But I'm going to miss you this weekend, I hope you know."

"I know."

"You do?"

"Yes." He looked down at his socks. "I know I haven't been saying much, but a lot has been on my mind. This is only my second time going hunting and well, you know..."

He looked back up at her.

"And?"

"I wish Dad was going with. I know that is crazy because he can't. He never could."

She turned to face him, crossing her arms, eyes moist.

"I'm thinking of not writing him anymore, too."

For an instant, she felt a shudder start at her shoulders and move towards her heart. She nodded and held him in silence, cradling his head on her shoulder. A hot, angry tear trickled down her cheek, which made her clutch him tighter. "You are going to have a good time, you hear me?"

She pulled back and put her palms on his shoulders, glaring into his eyes.

"Speaking of that," he said, glancing towards the clock on the wall, "I better get going. Josh and his dad will be by any minute."

"Everything packed?"

"Yes. Socks, pants, sweatshirts."

"Long johns?"

"Mom!" He squirmed.

"Just checking. You're free to go now." She smiled and waved him off.

She resumed cleaning up the rest of the counter and after wiping her eye one final time, loaded the dishwasher with pans.

Chase reentered the kitchen with his suitcase, rifle case, gym bag and the paper bag his mother set aside for him.

"Good luck, now. Have a good time," she said, hugging him another time before leaving.

"Thanks. I will." He slipped on the final sleeve of his jacket. "And check into this—you never know what could happen..." He continued, tapping on the neon green sale flyer now on the counter.

"I will."

She gave him a warmer smile this time.

A knock at the front door ensued, and upon opening it they found Josh, waving. "Hi, Ms. Krause. Ready, Chase?"

"Got it all together. Let's go."

Chase turned back towards his mother, who gave him a final hug. He hoisted up his rifle case and slung it across his right shoulder. Snatching his suitcase up in one hand and scooping up the mysterious paper bag in the other, he left to stow away his belongings into the back of Josh's father's truck. Josh picked up Chase's gym bag and waved goodbye. Karen waved back and watched as they left.

Neal waved, too, as he backed the truck out of the driveway and into the street. As the truck pulled away, she shut the door like a whisper. She then stopped to tug taut a stray strand of hair, staring at it to see if it had turned gray yet.

Chapter Five

In two separate trucks they traveled, until they would be a scant thirty miles south of the Canadian border. In all, it would be a six-hour trip. Neal drove now with Chase and his own son Josh, while Neal's brother, James, drove the pickup behind them. James carted the tents, the cooking equipment and the bedding—but the rifles and clothing remained with Neal.

Neal's stature was imposing, even hunched over the wheel of his new truck. A former high school running back, he had taken on a construction job after graduation and worked his way up to the top of the company, adding what looked like an inch a year to the circumference of his biceps. Although Chase never heard him brag about his income, one look at the chrome on his new truck did all the talking for him.

Josh sat next to his father now and Chase sat on the end watching the road for signs of glowing amber eyes in the ditches. Josh leaned back in the seat, until his father startled him.

"So how are classes, Josh? Keeping your grades up?"

Straightening his back, Josh inhaled deep and let out a sigh. He stuffed his hands into his pockets as if to dig for an answer written on a hidden piece of paper. "Yes," he muttered. "Physics is a bear, but I'm plowing through it." He then leaned over and whispered in Chase's ear, "And calculus is downright wicked."

Chase knew the courses were a horrid fit for his friend's wishes and abilities, but who wanted to hear that?

"Keeping up with the work?" Neal asked after a moment.

"Yes, but it is a heavy load at times." Josh reached out to the heater switch, flipping it on high for distraction.

"Are you picking a major soon?"

"I'll know soon. I'm just looking at the options right now." He pulled out his right hand, readied to nudge Chase with his elbow.

Chase looked over at Josh, who turned towards him as if to silently scream for help.

"Looking at options is good," Neal muttered, his tone of voice sagging like a deflated balloon.

"So where did you put my tree stand this year?" Chase broke in, allowing Josh to deflate his shoulders.

"Further back this time, near where I'm going to put my own. Sound better to you than last time?"

"Last time you were so close to camp that you could hear the tent getting zipped up. But Chase is a pro now, Dad. It's time for a real man's tree stand," Josh added, smiling and apparently grateful for the change of subject.

"How far back is yours?" Chase asked Neal, aware Neal was using a collapsible mobile tree stand.

"About a mile and a half is where I have my spot picked out. But don't worry. Yours is all taken care of."

Chase was glad Neal and Josh took the time a week ago to build him a stand in the trees. Typically made of loose timber, the stand was a row of three-foot-long logs nailed together, making a platform ten feet up in the air. Logs nailed between the tree trunks served as a crude but sturdy ladder. Neal seemed content with the portable version, which looked like a folding chair with a clawed metal collar on the back of it. The collar's teeth then wrapped around the tree trunk, digging into the bark for support. Chase always thought the portable model resembled a suspended deathtrap.

Neal pointed out the change from a clear, star-crowded sky to one with a low deck of advancing cloud. "Let's check the forecast," he said, calm but obviously curious. He clicked on the truck radio, twisting the tuning knob until an unfamiliar talk station came in.

"Light snow possible tonight, clearing by tomorrow. Lows in the mid-twenties."

"That's a relief," Chase said after a moment. "A dusting of snow means good deer tracking."

Josh yawned. "Did you remember to bring the cheap shells that Uncle Jim got you, Dad?"

"Discounted, not cheap, Josh. And yes, I did bring them."

Josh turned to Chase. "You've never met my uncle, have you?"

"No. Wasn't he in the army?"

"Used to be about ten years ago until the accident."

"Was he in a war?"

"No, he got hit in the leg when a field gun backfired and exploded. Killed a private," Neal chipped in.

"What does he do now?"

"Works in a sporting goods store in Saint Paul."

"He still hangs out with his army buds, right?" Josh asked.

"Not much anymore. After some of them ended up in the Gulf War he's had a hard time facing them. It's like he doesn't consider his leg scars a real injury, at least not a war injury like a real soldier gets. Or so he says. Whatever that means."

"What was that?" Josh asked, turning his head to look out the passenger side window.

"Where?" Asked Neal. "Back there. It looked like a truck on the shoulder of the road."

"Was somebody in there? Maybe we should help them," Chase added.

"No. I didn't see any lights on." Neal replied.

"So? If they're stranded..."

"Or waiting in the bushes to jump you...you can't be too careful nowadays," Neal countered.

"Maybe it's a couple and they're...you know...busy."

"What did you say, Josh?"

"Um. Nothing, Dad."

All three sat silent for the next couple miles. Josh then said, "Did you bring the pigskin, Chase?"

"No, I thought you did."

"Chevy, this is your responsibility."

"Mack, it is yours."

"Well, either way, here's the snow."

Neal clutched the steering wheel tighter with the onset of the snow showers. But the shower was brief, as a faucet that had been turned on for only a minute.

Chase then watched as a smile burst across Neal's face. According to the last road sign, there were fourteen more miles to the city of Virginia, and Chase hoped they would stop before setting up camp. He was sure he was not the only hungry one in the truck.

21

"How's Jimmy doing back there?" Neal inquired, peering into the rear view mirror. Josh twisted around to see his uncle waving back.

"Looks good to me."

"We'll have to make sure he doesn't turn off somewhere."

"The programs didn't work, huh, Dad?"

Neal sipped off his coffee and swallowed hard. "They only work if you want them to, Josh."

* * *

Riding behind in his truck, James listened to the music on the radio that faded with the increasing distance from the Twin Cities. Inside of his trailer were two tents—one for sleeping and the other for cooking. After all, he and his brother learned to take two tents after a disastrous first year of hunting. Sleeping and cooking in the same tent proved not only to be cramped, but dangerous.

He trailed his brother's taillights into the night, still fascinated by the look of driving through falling snow. He watched the pavement, too, as the sidewinding snow gathered itself into hissing, hypnotizing shapes that snapped and struck at his truck tires. Shaking off the distraction, he straightened out the steering wheel. The inside of his mouth was desert dry, and he thought innumerable times about turning off into one of the small towns strung out along the way and stopping at a bar for a few minutes. Jim resented Neal for making him haul the trailer with the tent it in this time, but what was a little resentment between brothers?

Jim dropped ten miles per hour off his speed and waited until his brother's truck swung into a sharp curve laced with thick walls of Jack pines. Then, he turned off.

Chapter Six

"There he goes, Dad," Josh blurted.

Neal growled and slowed onto the gravel shoulder. He spun the truck around in pursuit, prompting Chase to clutch the door handle. Chase swallowed a mouthful of air but it felt like a rock wedged itself in his throat. Neal just beamed straight ahead, grinding his teeth.

For Chase, Jim began to remind him of the last days of his father at home. What began as a few drinks after work snowballed into a six pack every night of the weekend. His father never became violent, but any hint of disagreement became motive for a trip to the bar. And although his mother reassured him that his father "just needed to work things out," he knew better.

"Down that way," Josh pointed out to his Dad, spying a familiar pair of red taillights arcing down onto a frontage road.

"Got him," Neal barked, devouring the distance with his new truck's proud speed. Jim's truck changed course and barreled into the parking lot of a convenience store, whose sign out front struggled to illuminate an otherwise lonely street.

Jim's truck slowed to a stop, and after Neal pulled up alongside, they both turned off their trucks. Chase could see both men looking over at each other with eyes that shattered the window glass of tension between the two men. Both men got out of their trucks.

"Sorry. Didn't mean to lose you. I was going to stop and get some food for the rest of the ride up. I'm starving." Jim stood with his arms out and palms upward, meek as a priest giving praise at the altar.

"Thirsty, too, I'm sure," Neal snarled, leaning against the open door of his own truck. He glanced back at Josh and Chase, unable to gloss over the incident. "You two hungry?"

Both nodded in earnest since four hours elapsed since they left home. As they bounded down out of the truck Chase let out a breath and let his shoulders sag. The stiff nighttime country air smacked him in the chest like a mallet, filling his lungs with the sensation of having swallowed a swarm of needles.

"You two go ahead, we'll be right in. Pick out whatever you want. I'm paying," Neal continued, slamming his door closed.

Chase and Josh meandered into the store while Neal and Jim carried on about Jim's stunt gone awry. Josh looked back, peering over a rack of potato chips, as if trying to read his father's lips. The only words the two had heard before going into the store were "Now let's not start it out this way..." Chase watched a minute longer, knowing Josh could probably replay the rehearsed pantomime outside almost verbatim in his mind.

After Jim and Neal finally entered the store, they perused the store's three aisles and then joined the others at the cash register. Jim looked on at a bag of beef jerky Chase had set onto the counter as Neal stared at a deli display of fried chicken. The cashier began heaping the pieces on display into an insulated foil bag as Jim went to get a package of jerky for himself.

After Neal paid, the four men returned to their trucks. Neal let Jim lead the way for the next thirty miles to no one's amazement.

When they came upon the splintered wooden gate that marked the dirt road that led to their campsite, all hints of sadness were shaken off. Josh spotted three deer some four miles from the dirt road, yelling first at the sight of the glowing eyes in the ditch off to the right, then at the sight of the deer themselves. Chase felt his heart rate increase as hopes for tomorrow's opener began to rise.

* * *

Six miles down the potholed dirt road that snaked and rollercoastered its way through the pines, the two trucks came upon a fork in the road. Jim slowed his truck to a crawl and then stopped. Neal stopped and waited as Jim backed the two-wheeled trailer into a clearing off to the shoulder and parked his truck. All four men bounded out of their trucks and surveyed the site. Although Neal and Josh laboriously cleared out the site the weekend before, it was now covered with a fresh powder snow. Chase watched as the others took in the view for a moment then turned to their work. He decided to look longer, however.

The sky this far north inspired Chase to think of it as a painting that took thousands of years to complete—each world a brushstroke of genius. Astronomers say that it is the dusty edge of the Milky Way that you see this far outside of the city, but Chase just thought of it as magnificent. After panning the heavens he turned towards helping the others unload the equipment.

Josh unloaded the cooking tent first, which was rolled up into a tight coil and stored in a long, plastic bag with handles. He pitched a bag full of stakes out of the trailer, landing it adjacent to the bag on the ground. Next came the task of unfurling the tent, then the sounds of muscle crushing metal, as the stakes smacked against the hardened earth. In the flood of the light from Neal's headlights, it looked to Chase as if they were driving stakes into a landscape paved with crushed diamonds. *Or the dust of billion powdered stars*, he thought.

With each crack of the hammer, each tug of the support poles, slowly the tiny city amongst no cities came to life. Neal gave a hearty cheek-to-cheek smile as the last support for the sleeping tent was adjusted and secured. But for all the hard work, for all the poles uplifting the tents, Chase could not help but think that one harsh gust of wind could launch the tents into the trees. Jim began unloading the sleeping bags from the inside of his truck and he emerged now, arms full and standing by the tailgate.

"I bet everyone is happy to see these," he said. His husky voice matched his squared shoulders and his thick, but short, coffee-colored beard. Chase grabbed the bundle of blankets and sleeping bags, embarrassed that someone did not rush over sooner to help.

Jim then extended a hand to shake. "You're Chase, right? Sorry about the confusion back there. Name's Jim."

"Nice to meet you," Chase replied. He worried after seeing the limp in the old sergeant's gait that Jim needed more assistance that he was getting. But Neal or Josh did not seem worried.

"Here," Uncle Jim tossed the remaining bundle at Chase, who caught himself staring. Jim then let out a snort of laughter. "You okay? You look like a deer that got caught in the headlights."

"I'm alright," Chase mumbled, laughing along as he paced back to the tents. The zipper door of the sleeping tent was open, and Chase saw movement inside. Josh finished batting down the last corner of a huge foam mattress, which was used to insulate the sleeping bags from the icy, rocky earth beneath. He had already thrown down a cobalt blue plastic tarp beneath the mattress since the snowpack tended to melt and seep through any holes in the flooring.

Neal meanwhile slid a portable foldout table into the cooking tent, struggling to see in the shadows cast by the larger silhouette of the sleeping tent. Fully erected, the table stood two feet by four feet across, with two foldout benches on either side. Neal then propped open all forty pounds of its supposed portability.

Chase unrolled the sleeping bags with the benefit of the better illumination that Neal had. Uncle Jim hoisted out two kerosene lanterns from his truck and delivered one to each tent.

"Give me your keys, Neal. I'll go shut your lights off," he said, extending the lantern by its loop handle. Neal then lit the lantern and helped unload more bags from the truck.

Josh and Chase then dragged a propane canister out of Neal's truck and attached a heating element to the top of it. The element looked like a red-hot electric sunflower when lit and would burn for hours to keep them warm throughout the night. Uncle Jim then brought the heater into the sleeping tent and lit the element. He then proceeded to unlace his heavy winter boots.

When the blankets were set in place in the sleeping tent, and the tables and cooking stove erected in the cooking tent, Neal zipped the cooking tent door shut, having turned the kerosene lantern to off. He then stashed all the rifle cases and cartridges underneath a black pullover plastic tarp in the closed back of his truck.

"Ready for tomorrow?" Uncle Jim opened. "Should be good weather out. Didn't you say you saw a lot of sign up this way last weekend?"

"You bet. Dad saw some near the path. Looks like one bedded down nearby, too," Josh replied.

Chase undid his own heavy waterproof boots, which were insulated well enough to withstand temperatures of forty below zero. Chase knew that one thing that could do a hunter in faster than anything else was cold feet, or worse yet, wet feet. He kept on his lone pair of cotton socks but tomorrow he would sport two pair—one cotton, one wool—because sweating had to be taken into consideration when hiking back to the tree stands.

"Hopefully this year you'll get one, Chase. And no more dropped bullets, okay?" Josh kidded. Smiles broke across all four of their faces, as a wave of hope and humor swept the room. Every year offered new chances and one good shot could erase all the memories of years without a deer, especially a first deer. But more than the deer hunt, though, they were genuinely happy to be together now—away from school, from their jobs and the zaniness of civilized routines. It was a time they could let their beards grow, and nobody complained to the other about not showering for a day or two.

"Got the alarm set?" Neal prodded his son, who was unzipping his jacket, happily adjusting to the flood of heat radiating from the propane element.

"Alarm clock? I thought you brought it."

Neal glared back. "You were supposed to bring it. I asked you to grab it before we left."

"Relax. I was just kidding. It's right here." He thrust it out to show his father, its green glowing numbers casting their own shadows. "I'll set it for five in the morning."

"Make it four-thirty in case you nail the snooze button. Better yet, make it four."

Josh thumbed the set buttons on the tiny white alarm clock. "Five o'clock it is."

Breakfast would be the first priority of the morning and Chase and Neal had been elected for the cooking positions. Like it or not, Chase ended up doing it by default, because everyone else figured that since he used to work in a restaurant, he had to know what he was doing.

Chase rooted through his bags and then turned to the curled up brown grocery bag his mother had packed for him. Unfurling its top, he plundered its contents, discovering candy bars, crackers, and two cans of pop. The gesture sparked a wide grin across his face, but further investigation unearthed a short note and a tiny, bundle of tissue paper. Carefully he unwrapped a tiny wooden deer carving. It fit neatly in his palm as he read the note from home.

Chase,

Just a note to let you know I love you. Have fun! Hope you liked the carving. I have a feeling you will get one this year.

Love—Mom

Warmth rushed through his cheeks and across his body as he tucked the note back into the bag. He did not know what to think of the trinket, as he set it back into the bag—at least not now. But the well wishes from his Mother and the hopes for tomorrow would stay right next to his heart.

Chapter Seven

Suddenly, Chase heard a hand slap against the electronic squawking of the alarm clock. He opened his eyes and watched as Neal went through a fit of yawns and stretches and then got up. Uncle Jim turned onto his side, but looked like he wanted to squeeze another five minutes out of the morning.

Next came a shake from Neal's bulky arm. "C'mon, it's time to go," he whispered.

Chase nodded and forced himself to sit up and shake off his slumber. He noted Uncle Jim was rolling around and laughed at the mumbling coming from Josh.

"Tell me again why we have to get up this early," Josh asked.

"So we can make it to the stands by dawn," Neal replied, slipping on his boots.

"Oh, that's right." Chase did not know if Josh was talking to himself or what because he was so out of it. Neal zipped open the tent door but no cold rush of air came in. He zipped it shut and Chase listened as the crunching and squeaking of his boots faded then disappeared.

"Get up, Josh. I'm not cooking for nothing you know."

Mumbling again, Josh rolled over under the attack of constant poking at his shoulder.

"Acceleration is the speed of velocity squared the distance."

Chase broke out laughing and then shook his head.

He slid on his boots at the edge of his sleeping bag, soaking up one last minute of warmth from the hissing propane heater in front of him. Unzipping the tent he plunged outside and smirked as the alarm clock was smashed into silence again.

Clear skies and the morning star greeted him as he wandered towards the cooking tent. In the deafening blackness of morning the outlines of the trees could barely be made out. The walk to the stands deep into the woods seemed tricky at best.

Chase entered the cooking tent. The kerosene lantern flooded the cooking tent with shadowy light as Neal clicked on the gas switches on the three-burner portable cooking stove. A match flung at the burners ignited them and Neal adjusted the knobs for a good, low flame. Chase watched as Neal withdrew a heavy black griddle from a paper grocery bag and set it on top of the burners. Neal then directed his attention to light another, smaller portable stove.

"Morning," Neal piped. "Drink coffee?"

"No thanks." Chase sat down at the edge of the foldout table. "So who is doing what?"

"I figured you could make the sandwiches and heat the water for the cocoa. I'll run breakfast. Sound good?"

"Sounds fine. Where are the pans?"

Neal withdrew a deep saucepan from another bag and added, "Water's in the big ten gallon jug outside near the back of the tent. It you need help, holler."

Chase nodded and stepped back outside. Upon returning, Chase lugged the black rectangular jug of water through the screened tent door and across the floor.

Neal began to pour powdered pancake mix into a plastic bowl. He then popped the lid off the cooler and withdrew a gallon jug of milk. He whisked up the pancake batter and set a carton of blueberries next to the big stove. He then slid a package of bacon out of the cooler and slit open the wrapper. He began laying pieces of it across one half of the griddle.

"Can you give me a hand for a minute?" Chase motioned towards the dead weight of the water jug, trying to tip some of its contents into the pan.

"Hang on. Here."

"Thanks." After the water flowed into the pan, Chase refastened the plug on the jug. He then set the pan on top of the lit burner of the smaller stove.

He then reached into the open cooler and pulled out a package of sliced turkey and a package of cheese. *Bread would be in the grocery bags off to the right, as would the plastic sandwich bags*, he thought. The bacon on the griddle began to pop and crackle, its edges beginning to shrink and curl. The smell was so tempting that Chase was sure it would wake the others. He then lofted a loaf of bread onto the foldout table and began to set up an assembly line spanning across three paper plates.

Rustling could be heard in the neighboring tent as well as excited but muffled chatter. Neal flipped the bacon with a fork and pushed the grease into the drainage channel encircling the griddle surface.

"Does everybody like turkey and cheese?" Chase asked.

"Far as I know. Great morning outside, huh?"

"Clear as a bell. Are the others getting up or just talking over there?"

"Jim! Josh! You up in there or still getting your beauty sleep?"

"We're up. Hey, we were up before you. We were just pretending," Jim jabbed back.

Neal smirked as he pulled the first strips off the griddle. He set them onto paper towels to squeeze out the remaining grease. Chase stacked the sandwiches together and breathed in the sweet smoky haze generated by the bacon.

Neal then dropped a wedge of shortening on the griddle, and Chase watched it skate across the surface and change from an opaque white to a clear, bubbling liquid. He scooped out the pancake batter onto the griddle and let it spread out into white discs. Plucking out a mitt full of blueberries, he sprinkled them across the cakes. As the edges began to dry and bubbles began to surface and collapse, he flipped them.

Chase heated water for cocoa, which in turn would be poured into everybody's thermoses. It was the best drink one could have in the tree stand since it kept you warm inside and did not run straight through your system like coffee did. He got up to return to the sleeping tent to get the thermoses when Uncle Jim stepped inside.

"Morning, boys," he barked, clearing his throat after the gruff hello. He stepped over to check on the heated water. Chase continued to walk on towards the sleeping tent, bumping into Josh, who continued to assess his alertness by rubbing his face and drawing his fingers through his tangled hair.

"Ready for your first one?" Josh opened.

"Hope so. You ready?"

"Always ready, always ready." Josh stumbled the rest of the way and shook off the groggy morning yawns with a grin. Cheer was

31

contagious now and Chase stepped into the sleeping tent to retrieve the thermoses.

The heater element burned on, but would be extinguished as soon as all had dressed for the day. The blast of heat from it invigorated him until he reemerged into the unforgiving Minnesota winter.

Neal served up the pancakes and bacon and as Chase reentered the tent, Uncle Jim poured syrup onto his own heap of cakes. Chase set out the thermoses and ripped open eight packets of cocoa mix, dumped them into the water and stirred it all together with a wire whip. Last night he resented being picked without a choice to do the cooking, but today he was happy and would not have it any differently. Several years elapsed since the last time he hunted, and now any contributing role felt like a big one.

"Neal, I hope you brought the buck scent this time. I think I forgot mine," Uncle Jim said, in between forkfuls of dripping purple blueberries.

"He brought plenty. What do you think made the pancakes taste so good?" Josh broke in, locked in a race to clear his plate first.

Chase laughed. The smell of buck scent even crossed his memory—a strange odor that smelled like a deer peed into a bottle of men's cologne. It drove the bucks mad and if you wore enough of it, they would even do a full-antler charge at you.

"Dad, gimme some more of them buck cakes," Josh kidded as he extended the plate towards his father, who was just eyeing the five golden brown cakes on the griddle for himself. Happily he plopped another pair onto Josh's plate and then served himself. Chase's plate was already at the table and he would devour the stack as soon as he finished topping off the last of the thermoses.

It would remain a morning of great anticipation as the men ate by the kerosene sun and listened to the background music courtesy of a Fort Frances, Canada, radio station. The real sun would inch its way up to the horizon soon, however, and so their tempo of motion increased.

After Chase and Neal finished eating, the lantern was doused, the burners extinguished, as all four men returned to the sleeping tent. Chase distributed the sandwiches and cocoa and Neal dressed the fastest, in order to return to his truck to fetch the guns and ammunition. Two pairs of socks for everyone. Two shirts. Blaze orange vests or jackets and orange hunting caps. Candy bars and now ammunition packed. Doused the propane heater and it was time to leave camp, filled with hopes, ambitions, and the chance to build new indelible memories.

Chapter Eight

Paired up and marching down the path that snaked through the wilderness, a faint, but detectable change could be perceived in the lighting of the sky. Even though the once indistinguishable silhouettes of branches sharpened, the four men wielded flashlights. Neal and Uncle Jim walked out front, forging through the new snow, their rifle cases in hand. Josh and Chase stayed twenty feet back, busy with their own conversations and lugging their own bags and rifles.

Chase watched as Neal and Uncle Jim crossed over two fallen trees strewn across the path. Uncle Jim hobbled across the logs, struggling the worst over the final one. Chase became aware of his condition again and whispered, "Will he be able to make it into his stand? He looks like he's having trouble."

Josh spoke in his normal voice. "Oh, him? He's fine."

Chase slammed his index finger across his lips. "Not so loud! Can, I mean how does he climb the tree?"

"It takes him extra time, but he still makes it. He's an excellent shot, though. Best out of all of us."

Neal and Uncle Jim marched further ahead, their muffled laughter a dimming beacon in the fading darkness. By now the sky color had changed from a midnight blue to a deep indigo and a breeze strong enough to lift stray fall leaves appeared. As Chase and Josh rounded the bend, Chase noticed a fork in the path ahead. Neal stood waiting for Chase on the left side and Uncle Jim stood on the right side of the fork.

The two men proceeded some two hundred feet down the path, just past the dip to where a large red ribbon was tied to a branch. The ribbon marked the beginning of a chain of ribbons and snapped branches which led to Chase's stand. Tingling like fireflies whirled and circuited through Chase's body as he approached, then held the ribbon in his chopper mitts.

"Do you want to wait until it gets light out? Or do you think you can make it?" Neal prodded, investigating the sky.

Chase glanced around the interior of the trees for the next ribbon in the line. He spotted it, and two more behind it. "I think I'll make it," he said, confident for now.

"If you're not sure, just wait 'til the sun comes up."

"No, no. I got it. You go on ahead. Good luck."

"Okay, good luck. Bring one home!" Neal waved him off.

Chase dove into the confusion of pines, aspen and poplar, temporarily regretting his ambition. Neal watched in concern for a minute and after confirming Chase was on his way safely, he moved on. Plodding on into the tangle of trees, Chase snapped more twigs, rendering a trail of dangling angles in the puffing wind.

The colors around him separated now as the sky turned a faded denim blue. He stopped, losing track of the next ribbon which led to the tree stand. Perhaps the stand loomed closer than he thought. Scanning the treetops, he eyed the suspended platform of logs some ten feet ahead. Approaching the stand, he set his bag and rifle down, and withdrew a long rope from the bag. Tying the rope to the bag handle would provide easy access to his things that would remain on the ground due to the limited, cramped space of the stand.

Straddling two Jack pines, the stand consisted of ten, three-inch diameter, knurled logs nailed side-by-side and suspended twelve feet in the air. A log ladder ran up between the trunks, but the dusting of snow on the stand and the ladder would impede progress especially when the snow became compacted and turned to ice.

Chase rested his rifle case next to the bag and withdrew four pieces of paper towel from his bag. Next, he dabbed the towels with a few drops of buck scent. After wrenching the cap back on tight, he pitched the bottle back into his bag. In the four compass directions some fifty feet from his stand he poked the towels onto stray branches, careful to be sure they were above his head. The smell was nasty, he thought to himself, but if it attracted bucks that was all that mattered.

Returning to the base of the stand, he hooked the looped end of the rope around his wrist and slipped on the shoulder strap of the rifle case. Scratching his head a moment, he marveled at the inefficiency of the stand's design. *How am I supposed to fit up there*, he wondered. All he could do was hope his treacherous climb would be rewarding.

Scaling the ladder, his foot slipped. He clutched the platform with steel fingers. One more slip could mean a nasty off-balance fall and nobody could help him. He sighed deep.

He climbed up three more steps, and then he hoisted his leg up. Although he contorted his body into a stable position, he felt like his whole morning dangled on the edge of a cliff. Once onto the platform of the stand, he had to straddle his feet around one tree trunk, with his back against the other. He let out a chuckle of relief, plotting out a better design in his mind that would certainly leave more room for maneuver. After all, one could only compact so many limbs in the equivalent space of a laundry basket. He was still grateful at the outpouring of effort and intent on Neal and Josh's part, however.

Hooking the looped rope onto one of the odd ends of a log, his attention focused on unpacking and checking over his rifle. Click. Click. In anticipation, he practiced aiming it at invisible running targets in the trees before him. Click. Click. *He's running*, he thought. Click. *Got him! One deer to bring back home.*

Straightening his back, he loaded, then rested his rifle across his bent knees. He listened, motionless. A crack. He turned around. It was only snow sprinkling down from the top of a
neighboring birch tree, with the clumps plopping onto the ground below. There existed an unearthly, profound silence up here—a stillness that forced one to listen to its beauty. A baby blue hue swept over the sky now, and the first sliver of the peach-colored sun erupted over the horizon.

He waited an hour, but was unaware of the passage of time until a glance at his wristwatch. There were stirrings in the distance again, and he raised his rifle once, but no luck. Chase began thinking how to overcome the lack of action. He thought about school for a few minutes, and how the pre-requisites took serious patience to endure. College had been a radical switch from high school—after all, no one cracked down on him for not attending class and no one reminded him about his homework. The absence of monitoring, though, also made him realize the hard way that if he skipped class, he would ultimately lose—in terms of money and grades.

Reaching for the rope loop, he unhooked it and pulled it up to the top in a smooth hand over hand motion. The candy bars inside the bag provided energy and the hot cocoa boosted his temperature, making the absence of motion in a stand tolerable. Tearing into a candy bar, Chase spotted the wood carving his mother sent with him now inside the bag. Smiling and reinvigorated, he pocketed it. He hoped she was doing well and longed for her to take her paintings to the sale in the mall.

The letter he had sent to his father was another thing, however. Click. Click. He practiced firing another round at an unseen target. It had been years since he started the habit of letter writing—years since there had been a steady reply. It had been years since the day he had arrived home from playing catch with Josh and he walked in to see his mother, silent at the kitchen table, head in her hands.

He recalled how she glanced up at him, but try as she did, she could not hold back the cascade of tears or the truth itself. She threw her arms around him, trying to sort out the confusion thrust upon the family. Kenneth Krause was gone—gone because of what she later found out was infidelity.

Kenneth disappeared down some nameless highway to a far away place, and although she did not explain the entire situation to Chase at the time, he eventually learned pieces of the sad truth on his own, but he never really understood the why. He remembered now his remark when he was thirteen: "I guess we were just another truck stop to him." His mother embraced and rocked him in an instant, crying and knowing that if anybody else would have said that, she would have backhanded them across the face. This was her baby, and she knew he was hurting worst of all.

Click. Click. The air-deer dropped to his knees. *A heart shot, easily.* Chase wiped away a hot tear streaming down his chilled, reddening cheek. He rested his rifle across his knees. He recalled now, too, how his father had left the day after taking him to a baseball game—their first shared trip to a game together—and ultimately, the last. Chase relived the anticipation, the smell of the hot dogs, the stair-stepping, sidearm-throwing vendors, the wave that the crowd did when the game against the Tigers got lame in the eighth inning. Although his mother had comforted him that he had done nothing

37

wrong, he secretly wondered even to this day if he had killed the relationship himself.

Chapter Nine

Little success was to be had this day, contrary to high hopes, skillful planning and the beliefs of Chase's mother. Chase unscrewed the top of his thermos, and checked it contents. He swirled the last ounce of liquid around in a vain effort to collect the last of the chocolate mud that sat on the bottom. Draining the serving cup, he slipped it back into his bag and finished his sandwich. The sun hid itself behind a layer of streaming cirrus clouds, which skated across the tops of the trees now like windblown cotton.

Time melted away under the warm wind of midday, and Chase could see some of the snowpack beginning to retreat into the earth. A check of his watch showed two in the afternoon, which was a good time to head in, considering nothing was happening. There had been two or three excited moments of tension, when a crackle and movement followed. Heartbeats drummed in his ears at these times, but no sighting of an actual buck meant no shooting.

Perhaps he was too close to camp or the deer were done moving for now. The vertical ruts on the tree bark he had seen near one of the ribbons on the way in was an excellent sign, however, because deer used tree bark to sharpen their antlers. Sign abounded near the main path, too, and Chase was sure somebody had luck today. A nearby gunshot earlier that morning gave him that hope.

Chase knew tomorrow presented another chance, but it still proved difficult to let go of this day. *If I stay another hour or even two—things just might turn*, he thought. *But maybe I have created too much commotion this past hour.*

He remained up top another hour, but then unloaded his rifle in disappointment, careful not to drop the bullet into the snow. *I've been a hypocrite, too*, he thought to himself. *I told Josh to get on with his life, but I cannot seem to let things go with my own life, especially with my Dad.*

But my situation is different, isn't it?
He resolved to go back to camp.

Chapter Ten

Bright orange flames rolled and twisted their way skyward now as the fire pulsed and swelled, spitting orange embers that wiggled their way through the air. Chase watched as Uncle Jim flung a last birch log down, nudging it onto the hottest portion of the bonfire with his boot. He rubbed his hands together, absorbing the warmth a few minutes before heading into the cooking tent to eat dinner.

Chase followed, and inside Neal finished panfrying hamburgers. Chase grabbed a stack of paper plates and handed them out. Uncle Jim seated himself on the foldout bench, crossing his arms. Josh sat down, too, but unlaced his boots in order to take a layer of socks off. With the real sun setting outside, the kerosene one overtook lighting duties for the night, throwing eerie shadows into every cluttered corner of the cooking tent.

"No luck for you, either, Josh?" Uncle Jim asked.

"Not a thing. Who fired that shot I heard early this morning?"

"That was your Dad. He didn't get anything, though. Told you you need glasses, Neal."

Neal continued to stir the baked beans in the saucepan. "At least I had a shot at something. Didn't see you hauling back no ten-pointer yourself, there, Jimmy."

He turned to the group. "Burgers are done. Chase, grab the bottle of ketchup."

Josh turned to face Chase. "We have to get Chase here a buck. You want to change spots tomorrow?"

"No, I think I will stay put. Too much sign in the area. Besides I have a feeling things will turn around."

"You sure? It's not a problem," added Uncle Jim, in between bites.

"No, it's quite alright." *There had to be something making all those tracks in the snow*, thought Chase.

The bonfire outside continued to snap and flicker, painting yellow-orange shifting silhouettes on the corner of the tent. Chase sat down at the table and Neal reclined on the cooler top as best he could.

Once Neal started eating, he became involved with his food rather than conversation. The cook remained the last to eat, and as always, apparently possessed the biggest appetite. Still enjoying each other's company, the four men remained optimistic, with no trace of sadness on any face. Josh began to stare, however, for a minute at a time at the assorted objects in the tent. Chase spotted the preoccupation and asked if he was okay.

"Just thinking. Thinking of new things to try tomorrow."

"I think maybe I'll go up a bit further back near the hill towards the end of the trail. They might be heading up that way," Neal added.

Uncle Jim just nodded and Chase continued to focus on Josh, perplexed by what Josh was really thinking about. He knew it had nothing to do with hunting.

Josh arose and dumped his plate into the plastic trash bag at his feet. Uncle Jim duplicated the motion and grabbed a hold of the tent door zipper. He began to unzip it until Neal stopped him. "Up for a game or two of cards, Jimmy?"

Acting like a caught thief, Uncle Jim scanned around the room to read the situation. "Sure, a couple games sound good." Neal continued to eye his food, stretching and expressionless, as if he rattled off rehearsed lines.

"Well are you going to take a seat? What's your hurry?"

"Just stepping out for air."

"You've had a day full of it."

"You're right. It can wait." He zipped the door shut and stuffed his hands in his pockets.

"Chase, grab the board. It's in the bag next to your legs."

Chase reached into another grocery bag and withdrew a cribbage board and a plastic wrapped deck of playing cards. He slapped both items onto the foldout table, as Neal dumped his own plate and rubbed his hands together.

Uncle Jim rejoined the gathering, tracing Neal's every movement with his bluish-gray eyes. Neal slit open the cards with a steak knife and took his own seat at the table next to Uncle Jim. "Teams?" He said, shuffling the cards into a gray fluid blur.

"Me and Chase against you two," Josh offered.

"Cut for deal?" Neal slid the deck to the middle of the table. Josh lifted off half the deck and frowned. High card dealt, and Josh held a two of hearts while Neal flipped over a four of clubs. Neal reassembled the deck and dealt out five cards apiece in less than a minute. Each man picked up their hand, and then Neal plugged two pegs for each team behind the starting line on the board.

Neal and Josh threw their one card apiece into the crib before Chase even finished arranging his cards. Uncle Jim tossed in his contribution a scant fifteen seconds later, leaving Chase alone on a novice island. It had been a year for him since he last played, and by the looks of it the competition would be intense and difficult. Clutching a lone king of hearts, he reluctantly set it on top of the crib. Josh would carry the team for certain, he calculated, while hoping his own two fives and two black tens would hold.

The starter card was a ten of hearts, and it took Chase two minutes to rework the totals points of his own hand in his head. He let a wry smile slide across his face, but let it evaporate when he witnessed Neal looking. Josh appeared worried, but Chase thought perhaps it was all a show. Josh started the round with a two of clubs.

Jim flicked down a nine, Neal a Jack of spades and Chase threw out a ten, making a total of thirty-one, and Chase happily advanced his team's peg two holes. After the round and the counting of the crib, Josh and Chase pulled into an early lead by ten points. Uncle Jim and Neal exchanged raised-eyebrow-looks of concern.

"Maybe we have ourselves a couple of ringers, here," Uncle Jim quipped. Neal turned his raised eyebrows to a new set of cards dealt out now by Josh with a speed equal to his father's.

To Chase, Josh winged the cards across the table in a blur reminiscent of a Vegas blackjack dealer. The green foldout tabletop emanated an aura of a Vegas table, with Chase's companions looming like gamblers getting their fix. Chase sighed and collected his cards with slippery hands.

In the end, though, as the last count of the cards in the crib would have it, Josh and Chase escaped with a two-point victory. Josh leaned back and smirked. "The student finally beat the master of card games," he mumbled. He shuffled the deck now with a confident slickness that suggested a cigar should be hanging off the corner of his mouth.

Chase watched the interaction between father and son at first with happiness and admiration. After a time, however, his shoulders began to sag. It was the kind of interaction he longed for, and as the final game progressed, at points it became painful to hear the laughter he could only imagine having.

At the end of the final count, Uncle Jim pushed himself up from the table, complaining his leg was killing him, and left to stand outside by the fire. Chase sprang up and toppled the lid off the cooler in search of a cold pop, hiding his face from view.

"That last hand was pure beauty, Pop," Josh congratulated.

"See? The master still has a few tricks up his sleeve."

"I'll say. Are you going to play some more?"

"No, I think I'll get a pop and go have a look at that fire outside." Neal sauntered over to the cooler but the approach caused Chase to swivel into an off-balance tumble onto the floor.

"You okay?"

Chase pushed himself up and rubbed his eyes as if there was dust in them. "Yeah, fine."

Neal snapped open a can of pop and stared at the jumble of dishes collecting near the stove. He fidgeted with a metal spoon, but eventually flung it into the bowl of unused batter from the morning. "The dishes can wait," he mumbled and it took him a few seconds to get a handle on the zipper. After leaving, his shadow passed Uncle Jim's on the tent wall and headed towards the sleeping tent.

Chase got up and sat down opposite Josh at the foldout table. Josh held onto the cards for a moment.

"You okay? Your eyes are red," he asked.

Self-consciously Chase rubbed them again, and ducked his gaze to avoid eye contact. "Fine," he replied. The cribbage board took on a double image for a moment as Chase wrestled back a tear.

"Ready to play another?" Josh asked, poised to cut the cards to see who would deal. Chase obliged and Josh dealt slower as if the competitive threat in the room had escaped like a shadow into the nighttime sky.

Chase clenched his eyes shut and recalled how all his letter writing was supposed to recreate the kind of bond between father and son like

Josh and Neal had. But it was not working. *No more letters*, he thought. *Whatta waste of time.*

Chapter Eleven

Karen Krause reclined on the sofa, bare feet propped up at one end, her pillow cradling her back at the other. Never susceptible to posture correction from others, she sank defiantly into the soothing warmth of her baby blue flowered comforter. She looked up from her clipboard and blinked thoughtfully at the picture of Chase resting atop the mantel of the fireplace. Why Chase had seemed depressed the night before worried her, but she hoped his mood would lift once he got outdoors.

The house seemed barren and lifeless tonight, as if it belonged to a stranger. It had been a frenzied Saturday, as the clipboard of papers on the sofa proved. There was a week to go before the school carnival and Karen volunteered long ago to organize it. As always, there remained problems such as the mini-donut vendor who continued to haggle over a working wage. Or the people scheduled to bring the fish house who remained unreachable by telephone.

At least the coloring contest would not fall through, she consoled herself.

She reflected on how her week was always filled with activities— PTO meetings, class curriculum planning, school fundraisers, and this month, dating again. But her weekends, as best as she could plan them, revolved around Chase.

Until now.

She had tried for years to find a suitable father role model for him to look up to, but her efforts led mostly to false hopes and dashed illusions. Steve Carson appeared to be the most promising long-term hope she had seen, but it was far too early to look past each date considering she had not even met his parents yet.

She stood up and opened the glass doors of the fireplace. She then lofted another birch log onto the sputtering fire and rolled it into place with the brass poker, irritating the embers from their slumber. She had

had enough planning for the day and peered around for a way to pass the remaining hour or two before bedtime. *Painting*, she thought. *Yes, the painting.*

Meandering over to her work she picked up the wooden palette. *A touch up seemed in order for the sky*, she mused. She unscrewed a tube of azure paint, squeezing out a marble size amount before mixing it with titanium white on the palette. As she tinged in the sky she began to reflect on the flyer Chase brought home to her yesterday. Was it selfish for her to try to go to the sale? She could not decide as she gave shape and form to the clouds on the canvas. *Chase had been concerned about his father and the endless stream of unanswered letters much more than usual*, she thought. The letters were supposed to evoke cheer in her heart, not anger, after all.

She dropped in highlights, mashing and twisting the bristles into the layers of paint to get the perfect tinge. She then set the paintbrush down, eyed her work from across the living room and smiled in satisfaction. *What do I have to lose by going tomorrow? Maybe it was an opportunity for change in disguise.*

She flicked on the television set, hungry for sounds other than self-created ones, and then cleaned the palette and brushes in the kitchen sink. After she returned from the kitchen, she burrowed back underneath the comforter on the sofa and waited for the weather forecast for the northern part of the state.

Chapter Twelve

"I am a hypocrite, do you realize that?" Chase said, making eye contact with Josh.

"What are you talking about?"

"The other day, I told you to get on with your life after Kelly broke up with you. That was cold."

"You're right. It was, but I needed to hear it." Josh sighed, as he sorted through his cards and pitched two into the crib. "But how does that make you a hypocrite?"

"Because I write to my father all the time."

"So?"

Chase let out a deep breath. He stared off at the kerosene lantern. "There's nothing there."

"I thought he sent presents at Christmas. And didn't you stop by his place last summer?"

"Sure I stopped by. But I think he visited me for a total of an hour in the two days I was there."

"That's cold," Josh said, shaking his head.

"No, that's old," Chase corrected.

Chase threw his two cards in the crib, sorting his cards with a vengeance.

Josh lowered his voice and his shoulders, crouching over the table. "Can I ask you something?"

"Shoot."

Josh turned his head towards the flickering shadows in the corner of the tent, then to the door, and back to Chase.

"I think I'm doing the wrong thing."

"With what?" Chase leaned back, studied his cards, trying to imitate a shark.

"School."

"How so?"

"I thought I was going to be an engineer."

"And?"

"I...think I want to do something radically different. But I don't know if it's okay."

"You mean okay with your Dad."

Josh inhaled deep and shifted his cards around, indecisive. "Yeah. I guess so. I don't know what he'd think. He pushed so hard for me to go to school and then with the help he gave me with the scholarships, he'd think I was doing him wrong if I quit."

Chase rolled his eyes, able to recite the pattern of the conversation in his sleep. It was, after all, Josh's trademark style of presentation.

"Are you going to quit or try a different major?"

"Not sure." Josh looked down at the table and then back up at Chase. "I want to get into acting or maybe even directing. You know, making movies." His shoulders seemed to relax now, like a mover who finished setting down the slate of a pool table.

Chase recoiled and swayed back, crossing his legs. His cards lay flat on the table now. "Acting? That is a huge leap. Do you have any experience?"

"I have been taking part in a drama club in school."

"Well, you always did collect videos." Chase crossed his arms, as if disappointed. "I guess I should have seen it coming."

"So, do you think it is okay? To tell him, I mean?"

"You'll have to or else you'll be one ticked off engineer. I'd hate to drive over any bridge you built." Chase laughed, and Josh smiled with his mock victory.

"Think about it. I could even do props. Designs, even. Think of the stage sets."

"I'm thinking, but feeling that you better tell you Dad before it is four years too late."

"I'm not like you, though, Chase. I didn't always know what I wanted to do with myself in life. You seemed like you always knew what you wanted to do in school."

"More or less..."

"I guess you are right. It's now or never."

"You haven't been indecisive. The more I think about it, the more I realize you just never admitted it. Do you still have some of those video tapes you used to make?"

"I think so, but I never thought much of them. It was just experimental crap."

"A crappy demo is better than a rickety bridge."

"Are you saying I can't be an engineer?"

"I'm saying you'd hurt less people building movies."

Josh nodded. "I'll take that as a compliment."

Chase shifted his gave as the giant shadows cast by the bonfire jerked. A hand reached out. Voices cursed.

"Do you think he'll blow up at me?" Josh prodded.

Chase remained focused on the disturbing play of the shadows. He lied. "He'll understand."

Josh nodded again, then rotated himself to watch, too. The interior of the tent fell into a paralyzing silence.

A fountain of flame erupted from the bonfire, brightening the walls and ceiling and darkening the shadows. Chase heard the distinct clink of a glass bottle on wood and flinched, as if to dodge the throw.

More cursing.

"What did you do that for?" Could be heard, loud enough to be heard back on the main highway.

"I didn't want this on this trip. Understand? We had an agreement," Neal scolded.

Josh shifted his feet, nervous and embarrassed. He kicked a bag by accident. "I'm sorry. I didn't think this was going to happen."

The monstrous shadows then froze, ashamed and aware again. A husky curse and mumbling could be heard, followed by one of the two figures heading into the sleeping tent. Chase figured it was Uncle Jim as Josh got up to leave for the refuge of the tent. Chase echoed a frown because he witnessed the frictions in his parent's marriage. Brothers, like Neal and Jim however, were bound to each other for life by blood.

When Chase and Josh came out, they came upon Neal, standing with his hands hibernating in his pockets. Neal smiled and tried to ease the tension. "Sorry, but I just didn't approve…" His voice trailed off.

The three men encircled the fire, standing silent for the next few minutes. One by one, as if imprisoned by the innumerable tree trunks of the forest, the two youngest hunters walked into the sleeping quarters. Chase looked back to see Neal, solemn and pensive, proceed to scoop dirt and snow in slow, heavy throws onto the fire before going in.

Inside the tent, Uncle Jim snored in the corner and Josh set the alarm again.

Then both Chase and Josh undid their boots. As Neal entered the tent, they burrowed underneath their respective comforters. Josh remained awake for a few minutes, but stared up at the ceiling as if staring into the coldness of outer space.

For Chase, the glossy-smooth memories of his second hunting experience washed away now, swept downstream to reveal realities jagged and as coarse as the walls of a canyon whittled down by the centuries. Tonight he clutched the tiny deer carving packed by his mother, almost dwarfing the promise of the real thing. He peeled off the silver wrapper of a candy bar and chewed it slow as he reflected. He knew things just had to change tomorrow.

Chapter Thirteen

A good sleep and early morning grogginess have a way of healing wounds and rifts, or at least distracting one from them. Neal again served breakfast, hurling plates of eggs and sausage links with flair and precision. Chase meanwhile stuffed sandwiches—happy just to get them into the tiny plastic bags without struggle. Chase hoped he did not double up on cheese or ham in anybody's sandwich and retraced his steps. Bread, ham, cheese, bread…he repeated to himself.

To Chase, it appeared that hope again began to permeate their thoughts, flushing out the remaining ghosts of anger lingering from the evening before. The sun, however, would struggle this morning to rise and burst through the building cloud cover, delaying dawn. Josh burst the silence in the tent with a question on whose turn it was to bring the toboggans out that morning, in case someone bagged a deer and needed to haul it through the snow. It was decided by committee that Chase and Josh should cart the plastic sleds.

The radio remained off this morning, however, and Chase began to wonder if he should switch it on. He knew neither Uncle Jim nor Neal had a CB radio or a cell phone in their truck, and so relied on instinct, broadcast radio, and sky watching to beat out adversity. He took their apparent lack of concern as a sign that maybe he had nothing to worry about, either.

The four men filed out of the tent after breakfast, plodding their way back into the sleeping tent to prepare for the hike back to the stands. Chase clenched his teeth as a sudden gust of wind ruffled his sweatshirt upon returning to the tent. It was a raw slap in the face of excitement, and as a result, he packed extra charcoal heating pouches into his bag as a countermeasure. Each pouch, the size of a tea bag, radiated enough heat when squeezed to keep the fingers and toes warm for three to four hours, and was essential when the action was sparse.

Josh exited first and Chase could hear him rummaging around behind the cooking tent for the sleds. Chase then stepped outside to see the sled ropes coiled up and encased in ice until several frustrated sledgehammer blows from Josh's fist broke them free. Josh then shook and pulled the ropes taut to unkink them and dragged them over to the edge of the path.

Uncle Jim wandered back into the cooking tent to locate a missing flashlight and after a two minute delay, turned on the radio. After another minute passed, he emerged from the tent, having rescued the flashlight. In haste, he doused the kerosene light in the tent but left the music on. The other three stood ready outside, their anxious paces mashing circles in the snow.

"You okay?" Josh asked.

"Yes. Flashlight rolled into the corner, that's all." Uncle Jim scooped up his backpack and plugged a pair of candy bars into it. He yanked the zipper shut, slung his rifle case over his shoulder and paired up with Chase for the hike down the path. Josh and his father stood five feet ahead, and when they were satisfied that everyone was ready, they left for their stands.

Chase could still hear the radio in the cooking tent, and how the Fort Frances station's disk jockey clipped off the final notes of a song with talk. He heard something about a storm, but shrugged it off as he heard a list of towns he did not recognize. He then began to walk with Uncle Jim.

Uncomfortable with the walking arrangements, Chase struggled to keep the tension at a minimum. Uncle Jim kept perfect pace with him, gulping in the shocking air like a seasoned runner. As Chase toyed with the empty sled bobbing along behind him, topics for conversation burst and faded in his mind like lightning, only there was no thunder to speak of because each idea became more sensitive than the last.

"How's Andy doing?" Chase asked, thinking of Uncle Jim's son— a neutral topic.

"Doing good, doing good. Almost out of high school, looking at the Army after graduation."

Chase spotted a ray of pride in Uncle Jim's eyes, like the sun breaking through an entrapment by clouds. "Still playing pool, too?"

"Definitely. Got the old man's aim, but he sure shoots a wicked game of nine ball. Won two tournaments last summer."

Chase remembered watching Andy play at the pool hall he used to visit, stopping his own game in awe of Andy running the rack. Tenacious and gifted, a gambler yet not a foolish bettor, Andy toyed with most of his opponents and this night was no exception. A cool silence befell the surrounding tables, with each crack of the billiard balls audible as a whip but rendered a colored blur by Andy's whisper smooth cue stick. He used enough draw, spins, and angles to dizzy a physics teacher.

"Didn't he run three racks in one night?"

"Four," Uncle Jim corrected. "The owner gave him a free hour for bringing in the extra business." His chuckle faded as Chase focused in on Neal and Josh. Chase could hear Josh trying to bring up his schooling dilemma, but Chase rolled his eyes when the conversation veered off on a tangent. *An act worthy of a screen test,* thought Chase.

"That guy at work still giving you problems?" Josh prodded, glancing back at Chase who fired back a glance of disappointment.

"Who? Lewis? Had to let him go. Guy almost hit a gas main with the backhoe. My crew can't take that kind of risk."

In all the years Chase had known Josh, it was the same labored approach to telling his father anything. *If Josh only knew how Neal talked about his son*, thought Chase.

Neal shook his head, and turned to wave back at Chase, who arrived at the entrance to his stand. Josh waved, too, hoisting up the looped end of the sled rope.

"Good luck, guys. I think today's the day, Chase," Josh called out.

"Hope so," Chase replied, waving to Uncle Jim, who had reached the others on the path. Chase forged ahead into the forest, shining a thin dart of light onto the ribbons twisting in the damp breeze. The snow underfoot crunched and squeaked like twisting Styrofoam with this morning's drop in temperature. He jerked the sled rope free from innumerable snagging branches, sighing because he could not carry it instead. The morning and the woods seemed lonelier now, and why he did not know. The revived newness of hunting faded now, but he kept his head and shoulders tensed and hopeful for the slightest crackles of a deer stepping through the bushes.

Fresh sign smattered the landscape near his stand, accelerating his heart rate. In one careful smooth motion he deposited his bag and rifle at the foot of the twin trees, clutching the towrope in search of a secretive storage spot for the sled. A nearby bush had to do for the clumsy addition to his gear, as he was worried the blaze red plastic or any human scent on it would startle even the dullest buck. The scrape of the branches on plastic drove him to bite his lip, however.

A bass drum rhythm of blood carried on in his ears now, as he felt sweat moistening the lining of his mitts. In his anticipation, he nearly slipped off the icy rungs before setting foot on the base of the stand. The warm glow of dawn never came this morning since it was swept away by a tide of grayish-white clouds barreling along aloft. The hushed peach and orange of yesterday's sunrise seemed distant now, as Chase cradled the rifle in his lap, dropping a bullet into the chamber. Petrified muscles now caged his animated heart, and breathing shallow, he waited for a twig to break.

Chapter Fourteen

Two hours crept on by with no sign of activity in the surrounding wilderness. Then, two gunshots rang out. The echoes deceived Chase as to their origin, but he believed they came from the opposite side of the path where Josh and Uncle Jim were. Clumped flurries began to bumble out of the heavens now and Chase could no longer gauge the speed of the clouds overhead. After glancing around, then down to the base of the ladder, he decided to fish for his storage bag for food. *Perhaps I should have brought a book to read after all*, he thought.

Another half-hour dragged by and the flurries multiplied into a light snowfall. Visibility remained high and it was so silent that Chase could hear the quarter-sized clumps of flakes crackling onto the tree branches. As he devoured the final corner of his sandwich a stirring shifted the bushes to the left of him. Frozen with his rifle on his lap, he craned his head to spot the intruder.

Crack. A branch broke. Chase still found no answer. Although the snow clung now to the branches, the weight of it would not cause that sound. A minute passed, with each heartbeat pounding louder in his ears. Crack.

He thought his heart would detonate in his chest. Over behind a bush, some forty feet in front of him and slightly to the left, a six-point buck lifted its head. The buck stared in Chase's direction, as if the tree trunk that supported his stand was capable of making noise. Chase knew even the slightest scent of a human could scare the deer away, which is why his hunting party had rolled away their jackets and snowmobile suits in a trash bag crammed with pine needles a week ago. All the preparation of the past month had been for this very sliver of a chance in time. Chase stared at the buck, gauging his weight, his grace, and his every flick of the tail.

The deer took tiny steps ahead, his head hidden now from Chase's view by the trunk of a birch tree. He would have to come out into the open or at least out from behind the tree for Chase to get a clear shot, however.

Again the deer froze, examining the scenery in front of him. Chase knew by the deer's excruciatingly slow steps that he sensed danger. One shot is all he had, and slipping his soggy mitts off, he wished he had been schooled in the art of silent motion. The deer took two more steps, his rear legs obscured by the birch tree. Chase lifted his rifle, closing his left eye to aim.

Line up the bead in the notch, thought Chase. *The bead in the notch. C'mon...move out. Move out from there.*

His taut shoulders made his hands shake, throwing his concentration off and wracking his ability to aim. Snowflakes began to whirl about now, cutting into the number of trees he could see in the far distance. For an instant, the sky worried him, but no, he was too close to give up now.

The buck lifted his head, relaxed and took four steps into an opening between the trees. Chase reasoned there was thirty-five feet between him and his target and he aimed the gun for a point behind the shoulder. It would be a heart shot if he was lucky enough that the hunter or the prey did not flinch.

And then his fever peaked.

Chase's bullet plugged into the deer's side, likely nicking the heart. The buck jumped, then staggered, its front legs buckling in an effort to stay upright. Stunned, the deer stood for a moment, as if to analyze the remains of its ability, and hobbled off as fast as he could through the bushes.

Chase elbowed his way out of the stand, delirious with excitement, almost to the point of jumping out of the stand. The climb down had to have taken five minutes, he reasoned. Surely the deer would be gone by now.

A trail of speckled crimson snow would inevitably guide the way, though, and Chase could still see the white of the deer's tail. Bounding down on the ground he dove for his sled and jabbed his hands inside of his bag for a tie rope. Slipping the rifle into its canvas case he knew he was taking too long. He took one glance at the sky. The snowfall kept increasing.

Determined, he knew he must follow. He conned himself into believing he could have the deer back to camp before the snow got nasty. He knew he could do it alone. Or could he?

Chapter Fifteen

Karen reclined in a wicker dining room chair, eating breakfast and reading the first section of the newspaper. Flipping and folding the unruly pages, she settled her eyes on page four, following a tagline from a story on page one. A tiny rectangular advertisement in the lower corner lured her attention away, however.

It was an ad for the art sale Chase promoted after returning from the rifle range. *Same time, same place as the flyer, and plenty of time to get ready before the noon opening*, she thought.

Come on, though. Who am I kidding? She wrenched the paper to the next page. Finishing eating, she flattened the newspaper on the table and gazed out the window at the steely, overcast sky. A long look around the room made the furniture and the walls seem cold, strange and hollow. *What could go wrong in trying*, she mused. All the other weekdays and weekends were ritualized, with her time compartmentalized. Youthful dreams began to whirl eagerly now in the restless curtains of the window above the kitchen furnace vent.

It was fortunate, she reflected, to have found the ad in the newspaper. It was better than fishing the crumpled up green flyer out of the kitchen garbage. She finally conceded now, too, that the thought of displaying her work tortured her throughout the night. Tugging at a coil of hair, she ground her teeth at the sight of a gray strand. She got up and left for her bedroom.

Karen's room was painted a hushed peach, for she detested the wallpaper her ex-husband originally enjoyed. Several times over the years, she thought it would be easier to move away altogether from here, leaving memories behind. After witnessing so many children trying to adjust to a mid-year move to a new school district, though, she held back. Chase had friends here, and she did not want to take them away.

She withdrew a full-length khaki dress along with a white sweater and got dressed. She then pulled out her makeup box and perched it on top of the bathroom vanity. Squinting, she turned her face from side to side. Age blessed her features and she was always happy she did not inherit her father's tendency to look older than the calendar said he was.

After putting on makeup and her earrings she returned to the living room to wrap up her first snowfall painting in plastic. Cradling its wooden frame, she returned with it to the kitchen for a bag. Karen rooted through the closet for two minutes, but unhappy with her findings, she settled on a black, plastic department store bag. As she tucked the corners of the frame inside the bag, she stopped to put her hand to her heart, for it was racing.

Sighing deep, she stepped back into the living room. She scooped up her long, black winter coat and slipped it on. As she thumbed the buttons through their holes, she stared at the mantle of the fireplace— at Chase's high school graduation picture in particular. She had been so proud of him that day, and it thrilled her that he chose to go on to college.

She wondered how his trip was going, hopeful he had seen the tiny carving and the candy bars by now. He would have called to thank her if he could. A handful of flurries tumbled down outside now, and she fretted again about his safety. Neal knew what he was doing, right? Chase knew, too, and she reassured herself that her fears were simply growing out of his absence. Karen picked up the painting, knowing she would get used to these weekends in time.

The drive to the mall took twenty minutes, leaving her ten before the show started. *Just enough time to talk to the owner or the salesperson or whoever was running the show*, she reasoned. The parking lot was full of the typical crush of Saturday shoppers, and the dread of being noticed with such a clumsy package as hers paralyzed her in her seat. Panning up and down the rows of cars, she chided herself and slapped the steering wheel with her palm. *After all, managing a roomful of restless second graders had moments more trying than this one*, she thought.

Stepping out, she unloaded the painting and scurried inside with her chin up. As she entered the mall, her eyes immediately came upon a sprawling display of works similar to her own. A crowd of the curious circled about, with intentions unknown to her, and from the look of it, to some of the shoppers themselves. Tables and stands stretched up and down the length of the mall's main runway, recalling images of student art exhibitions. The size of the layout amazed and comforted her at the same time—and then she spied the organizer of the event.

He was a curly-haired man in his forties, dressed sharp in a gray, three-piece suit, tapping his pen on a clipboard in hesitation. His eyes appeared to survey the artistic universe before him again.

"Excuse me, sir," Karen prodded, waiting for an opportunistic break in his concentration. The man looked over to her, peering over his bifocals.

"Can I help you, ma'am?" He replied with impatient eyes.

She noted the name on his name tag: Jason. "Is this an open show? Because I have a painting and I was wondering..."

"Let's see it first," Jason replied, his eyes focused on the plastic bag in her arms. "Can't promise that I have room, though."

Karen peeked into her bag and withdrew the painting. Nervous but forward, she held it up for him, all the while gauging his reactions with a wary eye. She held it out, but the longer it took, the more people she noticed watching her and Jason.

He stood for what seemed like minutes, holding and examining her work. She could feel her cheeks becoming flushed with humiliation as her day hung on his every movement and reaction. He was not reacting, however, and it worried her. He walked over to an associate, who was busy plugging in lighting fixtures. Although she could not read his lips, she did see the woman nod her head yes.

In the same tone of voice he greeted her with he asked, "Okay. But do you really want to sell it?" His clipboard, snug beneath his arm and at his side, showed numbers, names and addresses from what Karen discerned.

"Yes...yes. But you sound concerned." She wanted to hug her work tight, almost pulling it close enough to her to wreck it. She felt like she was leaving her baby at a new day care center and she was not about to let a stranger look after it without answers to her questions.

"Look, lady. I've done enough of these shows to know it's going to sell, okay?" His gruff demeanor came out now, along with a clear

New York accent. He looked over at a wall clock in the mall and then motioned her close. He whispered into her ear, "If you sell it here, ma'am, you will never see it again." A compassionate edge entered his voice as he seemed to awaken to her naiveté.

Her eyes roved up and down the artwork displays spanning into the distance. She fretted at the need for haste in her decision, watching the crowds swell. Karen bit her lip. "Okay." She waved off the painting and he motioned her to follow.

After walking only ten feet from where they first met, he patted an open hook on the pegboard display. "This okay, ma'am?"

"Sure." She learned from Chase that line of sight would be important, and with her painting facing another open mall runway she knew that Jason was not giving her a line.

"And what's your name, sir?" She asked, leaning forward, arms crossed, to hear above the chatter of the crowd.

"I'm sorry. It's Jason. Jason Carver. And you are...?"

"Karen Krause. I'm a schoolteacher. Do I sign up somewhere?"

Jason finishing hooking the wooden frame onto the board. "Yes, right here." He flipped out his clipboard, scribbled out numbers and dispatched her fears with a smile.

"We do ask for a donation, if possible, to the local food shelf. It's not necessary, though." Jason thrust the clipboard to her and extended out a pen. A buoyant smile exploded across her face. Karen penned in the necessary information, including her phone number. She resolved to stay and observe the sale from a distance, curious if Chase was experiencing similar success.

Chapter Sixteen

The delayed crunches of the foot-deep snow underfoot made sounds like fists punching through ice. Chase arrived at the point of impact, amazed at the crater in the snow and the dragging tracks leading away from it. Flecks of crimson could be seen on the same trail, making tracking easy. He took a look back at the tree stand, which was about forty feet away now. As long as he had a trail back, getting lost was not a possibility, he told himself.

Thick, heavy flakes began to stick to the windward sides of the trees, and he looked around for a tree that could be used as a landmark in case he lost sight of the stand. The wind howled and whistled now in his ears, driving the apparent air temperature down with it. He came upon a giant birch tree, which would do for a landmark he figured. He recalled his father telling him to always look for an object that seemed out of place—such as the downed tree by where his father used to take him fishing by the river. On the banks of the Mississippi they used to fish for hours, at a secretive spot that was only accessible by a winding dirt trail and a two minute climb over a ridge of boulders.

His hands shook with excitement and his heart rate increased nearly to the speed it was at when he fired his kill shot. Walking next to the red trail, he was careful not to trample it. He hoped he would remember the way back to the stand, because following the ribbons out from there would be easy, even in the face of the driving snow.

The trail wound and snaked its way through broken branches and trampled bushes and over a small hill in the snow. Chase looked back to try and get a fix on the stand, but now it had slipped out of sight or blended in with the whiteness that seemed to take over the sky, the trees and even the footprints he was leaving behind. He reached out and began wiping the snow off the trees as he passed by them. As the sled grooved the snow behind him, he plodded along until he came upon the deer, collapsed and motionless in the snow.

His heart hammered at his ribcage as he poked at the grayish-brown mass with his rifle case. Approaching an inch at a time, he eyed the deer carefully, nervous that it could jump up and stagger off. But of course, it did not.

Chase prodded at the gunshot wound, and its frayed crimson, black and gray edges startled him. It really had been a good shot, and even an experienced hunter would admit that. He set his bag down and unzipped it. He pulled out a long rope, and set its coils onto the ground. Next, he pulled the sled up next to the deer.

Steam rose as snow battered the animal and Chase could feel the warmth that still radiated from the buck. Then, Chase did the thing he was warned not to do but did anyway: he looked the deer in the eye, and the deer blinked back. Chase leapt backwards, almost tumbling into a nearby snow bank. The others had told him that if the deer was still alive, the most humane thing to do was to shoot it again.

Chase gripped his rifle case, and unzipped it. *If it blinks again, I'll shoot*, he thought. *But he looks helpless now that I've knocked the wind, the grace and the spirit out of him. Maybe if I just walk away I can forget it all. No, I can't leave him here. Not now. Shoot. Why did I have to look?*

The buck's eye stopped moving and soon his chest did not rise to take in air. The woods seemed lonely now, as Chase remained still for a moment, watching the snow, the trees and the deer. He zipped the rifle case back up and threw it into the snow.

The once proud set of legs, that only moments ago had put up such a fight, seemed stiff as sticks now, and as Chase uncoiled the rope, he began to bundle them together. The blink of the eyes still saddened him as he lugged the buck onto the sled. He knew why it was so difficult to look them in the eyes now. He recalled Josh's father having to shoot their family dog after it had bitten a neighbor boy, and that was never easy for Neal to deal with. The memory of the eyes plagued him years later and Chase knew this incident would bother him much the same. He wondered to himself if deer even had souls or a place to go on to as he picked up his rifle and bag and began to pull the sled.

Then there was a pink flash that filled the sky, followed by a low, steady rumble. It was lightning, which meant the snowfall could only get heavier. He pressed onward, back down the trail, following the fading spots in the snow and the marks on the trees. *The others must be back at camp now*, he reasoned, as he stopped to zip up his jacket as far as it would go. *All the layers of clothing would prove their worth now*, he thought. *Wait until the guys see what I pulled in. Too bad Dad could not see this one.*

Chapter Seventeen

Chase wished he had a navigation device now as the blizzard made it impossible to see more than twenty feet in front on him. All of the jokes in the gun shop about the clerk who always talked about navigators suddenly did not seem so funny anymore. The trail, which minutes ago seemed reliable, began to fail him in the face of the scouring wind.

The weight of the buck on the sled did not make things easier, either. He did not realize it would take so many rest breaks just to travel what had to have been fifty yards. The deer slid off the sled twice already, complicating the situation further. He could feel his back muscles, worn and sore, under the stress of the rope and the thought of sweating worried him in between the cold blasts of wind.

So far, his father's aged advice on landmarks paid off. A sigh of relief swept over him as he came within sight of the birch tree that he committed to memory. The deer slid off again, but by the time he had it secured on the sled and then walked ten more paces, he was at the tree.

As familiar as the tree looked, though, the trail of blood and footprints did not look like he remembered it. He was not sure if his memory began to play a trick on him now or if in his original state of excitement he just did not pay enough attention. Perhaps it was even the wrong tree. He marched on, though, rounding the clogged trail of prints.

If only my Dad could see me now, he thought. He knew of course that his father never would. Kenneth never would see the joy on his face, never could hear the animation in his voice as he retold the tale of the hunt. Chase felt like a man now, having passed a milestone of sorts.

Yet the weight of the deer on the rope burrowed deep into his shoulder blade. He only looked up in brief spurts now, keeping his face down to avoid the sting of the snow. *The pain on my shoulder is worth it*, he consoled himself.

He had been thinking of school earlier that morning in the tree stand, and how the whirlwind of activity surrounding orientation had been so dizzying at first glance. *So many forms and applications, prerequisites and planning, advisors and then homework*. It did become easier with practice, however.

It seemed simple and natural, too, that his father should return someday, with arms full of presents and a head full of answers and stories in response to all the letters. Chase began to understand what his mother had discovered years before, however—there was no turning back, no matter how many wishes you made. He remembered now how his mother used to call his father, sometimes for days on end, until one day there came a permanent busy signal from the phone being off the hook. She tried again a week later but soon gave up.

Chase caught a glimpse of another birch tree in the distance, bringing a smile to his face. The trail at his feet almost vanished now, a casualty of the unholy war of ice and wind being fought around him. The deer stayed on the sled now, perhaps frozen in place, but he had to stop to catch his own breath. His knees ached out their awareness but he switched the towrope to the other shoulder and carried on.

Mom had made it, that was for sure, he thought. *Made it all this way without the phone calls.* He knew he had been hard on his mother at times, putting her through emotional torture when he stayed out late, and worried her with his poor, but now greatly improved, study habits. *Oddly enough,* he thought, *she seemed to act as if everything would eventually turn out okay.*

Chase arrived now at the birch, and slapped its caked bark in reassurance. He flicked the snow off the towrope, jerking the deer to a temporary state of artificial life. As he looked back, though, he knew the deer was dead. It was as dead as it would ever be.

Scanning the horizon he could not picture the tree stand ahead of him. Shallow imprints were all that remained in front of him, and having no choice, he followed them. For the first time now, fear began to set in because he could not remember what had seemed so clear an hour ago. Shoulders tensing, he knew that there might not be anybody that could help him now.

Chapter Eighteen

Josh looked up to see Neal and Uncle Jim staggering back to camp through the snow. He had been at camp for half an hour now, listening to the radio as he refastened a rope that secured a corner of the cooking tent. He already rested the doe he had shot and tagged against the snow bank behind the cooking tent, covering it with snow to both hide and preserve it for processing. The wind toyed with the tents, and Josh grimaced because Chase had been right all along—wind made their tents as vulnerable as tiny rowboats on the ocean.

Uncle Jim put his rifle and bag next to the sleeping tent, his cheeks windburned and sore. "This is crazy. I didn't hear about this in the weather report, did you?" He shouted above the wind, which made the tent walls flap like a gull's wings.

"No. Storm wound up near Fargo," Josh hollered back. He leapt up to help his father, content for now that his handiwork with the tent stakes would hold. Neal lumbered up to the cooking tent as Josh snatched his bag and rifle. Uncle Jim hurried inside the sleeping tent.

"Where's Chase?" Neal worried aloud, putting his hands on his hips. "Have you heard anything?"

"I heard a gunshot this morning from over your way. Thought it was you or him. He hasn't been back at all from what I can tell. I wanted to go looking, but I might need help if he's in trouble."

Neal surveyed the campsite. "We have to go looking for him. He'll never make it in this. Can't see past the road over there." Neal gulped and turned his head, struggling to breathe against the tyrant wind that was trying to cram his breath back down his throat.

"See you got a doe," Neal continued, motioning for Josh to head into the sleeping tent.

Josh nodded and led the way inside. Neal zipped down the door and listened to the radio, which Josh brought over from the cooking tent. Uncle Jim was already huddled around the propane heater.

"How bad is it?" Asked Neal, rubbing his reddened hands together.

"It's bad. Six to eight inches by nightfall. Winter storm warning for the area. Any sign of Chase?" Uncle Jim replied.

Josh just shook his head. The solemn heater element burned away at the cold, its hissing filling in the silence left by the men in the tent. Neal sat on the edge of his sleeping bag, head buried in his hands. After a moment, he lifted up his head.

"I'll go get him. Actually, me and Josh will go. Be sure to bundle up, Josh, after you catch your breath."

"No, I'll go," Uncle Jim countered.

"With that leg? You'll never make it if you have carry him. Chase has got to weigh almost as much as Josh here."

Uncle Jim stood up and sneered, "What are you trying to tell me? That I can't do anything?"

"Sit down. Don't get stupid on me."

"Who's getting stupid? The kid's out there freezing to death for all we know and you want to argue about who's got the better legs." The color of anger brightened his cheeks. In fact, it looked like he wanted to spit.

"I'll tell you this," he continued. "You know as well as I do that we both felt something maybe wasn't right this morning with the clouds moving like they were. If anything happens to him, you are just as guilty as me."

"All I was saying was..."

"Saying nothing. You know I can find my way through these woods better than you can. You may be my big brother, but you're getting too stubborn and proud for your own good."

"Are we going to fight or..." Josh felt the urge to swear, but held back at the look of surprise on his father's face. "...or save him before he gets killed?" Josh swung his arms upward. "Dad, Uncle Jim's right."

Neal twitched and twisted his lips, readied to explode.

"Well, I am right and you know it," Uncle Jim continued.

"Alright. You and Chase go. I'll secure the camp and get some water going. If he's frozen anything he'll need to get it warmed up right away."

Neal stood up, adjusting his snowmobile suit. "Bring some binoculars and sticks or ribbons to mark the way." He turned away a moment and glared back at Uncle Jim. "I hope he's okay."

"Me too, Neal. But we have to do what's best. Josh, get the binoculars. I'll find something to mark the way." Uncle Jim shook his head and sighed. He zipped his suit back up and refitted his hat on his head. Josh soaked up one last minute of warmth from the heater, but then began to chastise himself for getting as much heat as he did, knowing that Chase could only dream of it.

Binoculars in hand, Josh exited the sleeping tent. The intense snowfall subsided a bit, encouraging him for the moment. *But minutes are all hypothermia needed to do its damage*, he thought.

Uncle Jim left the tent, wincing at the wind that still took smacking blows at their faces and the tents. Neal then exited the tent and walked into the cooking tent where he began to put large pots of water on the cooking stove.

Josh then entered the cooking tent and grabbed a handful of charcoal hand warmers. He began to rub and activate them as Uncle Jim rooted through the tent in search of something—anything—to help them find their way back. Josh knew time and the cold were destroying their odds by the minute.

Uncle Jim began frantically plundering the grocery bags on the floor, tipping some of them over. He glanced up, "Any ideas Neal?"

"How about the roll of ribbon. Grab my compass, too."

"That'll work. Thanks." Uncle Jim dove over to another grocery bag, barreling his thick hands into its depths. Josh ambled over to assist, but Uncle Jim raised up his hands, smiling triumphant.

Neal lit the stove burners and set the pots on the floor. He returned outside to get the water jug. "Good luck, guys."

Josh and Jim nodded and marched out. Uncle Jim surveyed the trees and the sky. "Wish we had some flares. But I guess it wouldn't matter much in this."

Behind them, Neal prodded and kicked at the firewood from last night's bonfire. Josh knew there would be a slim chance at starting a blaze now, especially with all the wind.

Uncle Jim and Josh hurried onto the path, eyes darting around the landscape. Josh hoped Chase was on the path, but each step only cemented his blackest fears. "He could be anywhere, Uncle Jim."

"We'll find him, son. We'll find him."

"Think he got a buck?"

"Probably. None of us fired that other shot."

Josh peered through the binoculars, hoping for a short, simple mission, but white ghosts appeared and disappeared in front of his eyes. "What got into Dad back there?"

"He's nervous, Josh. Like the rest of us. But I know he can get overbearing sometimes."

"I know." Josh thought about school again, which was another theoretical mountain left to conquer in the distance. He had given thought to telling his father about his new goal, which really was an old goal pushed under in denial, or so Chase analyzed. He smirked, thinking Chase should be a counselor, not an architect.

"Does he ever badger you about school like that?"

"Sometimes."

Josh stopped to look through the binoculars. He panned the woods for any flashes of orange.

"There is something I have to tell him," Josh said after a moment.

"What?" Uncle Jim shouted about a gust. "Say again?"

Josh bit his lip, altering his thoughts. "It's hard to deal with him," he shouted back.

"That's for sure." Uncle Jim looked back, as if to see if he missed something on the way. Nothing, but a frigid blanket closing down for the day.

Chapter Nineteen

Cold and wind have a way of knocking the energy out of a person, lulling them into a dangerous exhaustion that turns their thoughts to sleep. Chase pushed the thought of slumber aside because he knew he had not made it to camp yet. His return to the landmark birch had not been triumphant, but rather tragic now. He gazed at his watch, pushing back his sleeve with numb fingers. With the lens of the watch fogged over, no bearing could be made on the reality of time.

The pockmarks in the snow that used to be his footprints disappeared now before him. The snowfall let up a bit, but an increase in wind kept visibility low. He sensed what a desert traveler must feel like, alone amongst the shifting sands. The trees themselves might as well be sand, too, he thought, because they were no help now.

He stopped and inhaled deep, feeling himself teetering on the edge of hyperventilation. *C'mon Chase, use your head,* he thought. *Perhaps I am only off a little bit.* Switching directions, he veered off towards what he thought resembled a snow-covered tree stand in the distance.

Why did I have to be so blunt with Josh, he thought. "Get on with your life." *How cold could I have been? I'm becoming a hypocrite just like Dad was. He used to knock the neighbor, Manny, telling him he drank for no good reason. Then look what happened to him.*

His heartbeat drummed in his ears now as a tingling ignited across his body. It was just him and his deer—a dead deer to be exact. The ground sloped down beneath him now, which was an unfamiliar sign.

Or would I rather be like Neal? Work all you life, make it to the top, only to have your son resent you. Or is it better to be like Uncle Jim? His life is basic—he works in a sporting goods store and goes home at night to his wife and kid.

But that's just it—his life doesn't appear to be going anywhere fast.

Just then his boots gave way into a patch of thinned ice. With a splash, he felt water gush in over the top of his boots, only to wrap around his ankles like shackles. Chase braced for a rush of pain, but it never came, which scared him into thinking frostbite already had set in.

Resting on the bank of what looked like a creek, he pulled off his boots, wringing dry his socks. *There had to be some other trick that his father never told him about*, he worried. *Some secret to getting out of the woods that only seasoned hunters knew about.* The memory of getting lost in the woods near the river as a kid came back now, with frightening relevance. He remembered getting turned around back when he was eight years old, screaming for his Dad to find him. Fifteen minutes passed before he was discovered sitting on the ground, bawling, and a scant twenty feet off the trail out of the woods.

Of course, he knew, his father would not be there to wipe away the tears this time. He shook off the blurriness in his eyes and got up, wincing at the moisture numbing his ankles and feet. *No one here to save you this time, buddy*, he thought. *Just me and this dumb dead deer.*

He panned around, trying to regroup his senses. Sleep seemed like a welcome option now. *If I could just lay down here*, he thought, *they would find me when the snow stops. It would be so much easier.*

Chase shook off the thought as crazy talk. He was vaguely aware he was slurring his words. His father knew so much about the world. Why did he keep it from his only son?

His feet punted away a dune of snow. Everything seemed so dead. The snow drifted like sand, but was void of life. The wind, the trees, the deer—it was all dead. Chase swung his fist at some invisible boxer, as he wrestled with the towrope that became snagged on a branch.

The whole mess started when I walked left from the tree stand kept going should have stopped and gone back to camp, he thought. His right shoulder throbbed in pain under the grinding pressure of the rope. The deer was killing his every step now and he knew it.

If I ever get out of here alive, he thought, *I'll never abandon my own kid, not for anyone, not for anything.* Staring at the sled, his vision blurred.

He let the towrope slide off his mittens, and the sled and the deer tumbled down an incline, coming to rest at the base of a fir tree. Forging on unhindered, his legs buckled twenty feet later.

* * *

Josh stopped moving, peeling back his orange hunter's hat to listen. "Did you hear that?"

Uncle Jim stopped also. "What?"

"I heard a noise. Like a thud."

"Probably just a branch breaking under the weight of the snow."

Josh nodded but did not agree. There was no familiar cracking sound to go with what he heard. He stared hard through the binoculars and found no comfort. The noise emanated from the left side of the path, clear above the din of the sandpaper wind. He wanted to split up to satisfy his hunch, but he knew it was a foolish course of action.

The two men marched on, approaching a fork in the path. Uncle Jim requested the binoculars, and Josh nearly refused. This time, Uncle Jim stopped first. He peeled back his right mitt and twisted the focus knob on the eyepiece.

"Now what? We're at the fork." Josh knew Chase's stand was off to the left, and Chase probably was, too.

"Here. Look." Uncle Jim handed the binoculars back to Josh.

Through the binoculars, a fuzzy orange dot at the base of a tree became a hunter's cap, and on that cap Josh could see a tiny black deer emblem.

"Start cutting ribbons, son," the old sergeant barked.

Josh pumped his fist and handed the binoculars back to his uncle. The sergeant pointed him to the spot to the left of the path. He tore his jacket pockets asunder for a pocket knife to cut the ribbon. Finding none, he gnashed off chunks of blaze red ribbon with his teeth.

Sergeant James Weldon secured the binoculars and forged ahead to the edge of the forest, pointing out a sturdy branch for the first marker. He then led the way into the trees, hands shaking.

Chapter Twenty

A jolt of electricity punched Karen Krause in the heart, but to her it was a familiar sensation. It meant something was wrong, either with a relative, or worse, Chase. She slipped away from her outpost as an observer at the sale and scurried down a mall side entry. Lunging for the payphone, she jabbed out the numbers and waited.

When her answering machine began its message, she leapt ahead to check for old calls. The machine beeped three times, indicating no new calls.

Hanging up the receiver, it felt like a hole began to open up right where her heart was supposed to be. She stared at the outside entryway, thoughts lost in the snowflakes tumbling down outdoors. *Chase has to be okay, doesn't he? He is with Neal and Josh and Jim, who all know their way around the woods better than Chase does.* She resolved to call her mother as soon as the snow ended.

"Ma'am? You done with the phone?" Came a voice from an eight-year-old boy with strawberry blonde hair and matching freckles. Karen turned to the boy, startled, wondering if his mother stranded him at the mall.

"I'm sorry. You go use the phone, honey. Sorry." Karen meandered back to the show, her arms crossed tight.

She wandered around the exhibits, occasionally stopping into a clothing store at the sight of a sale. The mall walkways appeared ready to explode under the crush of shoppers, and there was little room for Karen to wiggle through at times.

Looking back, she kept an eye on her work. Although it received attention, no buyers unhooked it from its perch. *Perhaps the price was too high*, she thought. Or maybe she was not good enough and she should dash away with it, keeping her humiliation to a minimum. *Perhaps it was...*

"I did not know you were into painting," came a soothing, deep voice from over her left shoulder. Karen spun around to reply as a smile gushed onto her cheeks.

"I didn't expect to see you here," she replied, a delicate hand covering her mouth.

"Well, I do run a museum, but I love to showcase works from local artists once in a while. This is yours, right?"

Karen blushed. "Yes, it is."

"Kind of an impressionistic work. I like the snow, and the trees going into winter. What do you call it?"

"Virtue." She watched his eyes a moment, searching for some type of involuntary inner response that would only surface in his features. "But I'm afraid it's not selling, Steve."

Steve stared into her eyes. He swallowed hard. "The price is a bit high."

Karen bunched and loosened her long blonde, curled hair, then drew it into a ponytail. "Think so?"

"I mean, it's just that most of this crowd here wouldn't know the right price to pay. They all look for cheap things. But I have an idea. How about we put it into my exhibit at the museum? There is a chance you'll never see it again if you leave it here. I know a lot of people who would have snatched this up hours ago, if they could be here."

"Steve, you sound pompous," she whispered. "But I appreciate the sincerity."

A smirk washed over her face.

"Sorry. Can I put it up in the museum, though? I mean, if you do not mind."

He unhooked the painting and began to walk towards the cash register.

"I don't mind. And yes, it's okay to try and get on my good side. Really." Karen kept pace but reached out her hand to stop him at the register. "But I'm taking it off sale first."

Jason Carver obliged and wished Karen the best of luck. The couple walked towards the exit. "How's your son doing?" She asked, having taken the painting from Steve's grasp.

"He's doing good. He's at his grandmother's house right now. How is your son?"

She turned to survey the snowfall. She hunted around inside of her purse for her car keys and maybe an answer.

"He's doing good in school."

Karen dropped her keys on the floor, and out of instinct, Steve bent down to retrieve them. She met him halfway as he forfeited the keys. "Thanks," she replied, waving goodbye as she pushed open the glass exit doors.

"Aren't you going to put your coat on? It's freezing out."

"I almost forgot."

She put on her coat, as quick as she could and then pushed the doors open again.

"Can I walk you to the car?"

"That would be nice, Steve. Thanks."

She clutched her coat tight against her sweater. She smiled to acknowledge Steve at her side, and then peered towards the heavens. Steve slid his arm under hers, hooking them together by the elbow. Karen yielded, pulling him closer.

"Is something bothering you, Karen?"

"It's nothing. Really. Just watching the snow."

"Where's your son, by the way?" Steve prodded. She could see that he, too, began to take on the look of a parent preoccupied with the welfare of their child.

"He's hunting."

"Where?"

"Up north."

Steve led Karen up to her car door. "He's not near the Canadian border, is he?"

"Yes, he is. Why?"

He took a breath. "There's a big snowstorm blowing around up there. Came up last night from the Dakotas."

Karen froze, firing off a glance hot enough to liquefy iron. She flung open her car door and plunged her key into the ignition. She kicked over the engine, letting the painting crash onto the floor of the backseat, and glanced over her shoulder for oncoming cars.

Steve bent down between the door and the frame. "Sorry, I did not mean to worry you so much, Karen."

"I know. I have to go now. Sorry."

"That's okay. I understand."

She looked into his eyes and sensed that he wanted to kiss her, but was suppressing the urge. "You do?"

"Yes. Now go on, go check the television." He patted the roof of her car and backed away.

A genuine smile broke across her face. "I will. Thanks for the offer on the painting. I'll keep it in mind."

"Don't worry about it. Go."

Waving, Karen wheeled out of the parking spot and onto the service road. Steve stuck out his thumb and little finger, placing his hand up to his ear and then pointed to himself. She nodded back and sped away, isolated again by her worry.

Chapter Twenty-One

Josh and Sergeant Weldon stormed through the icy brush only to find Chase face down in the snow. Josh noticed Chase's bootlaces were untied, widening his concerns that he had gone into hypothermia. He overturned Chase, grabbing him by the shoulder.

"Chase! Wake up, buddy. We're here. Chase!"

The sergeant pointed out that his face rested on his rifle case, avoiding direct contact with the snow pack beneath. Josh shook his shoulder again, brushing the snow off of his jacket and yelling his name. As Chase's eyes opened, the sergeant cheered, and Josh was thankful miracles still occurred on earth.

Chase's ear lobes were white, and his face remained drained of color. Josh tied up Chase's boots. "Think you can get up?"

Chase mumbled and blinked his eyes. "Think so. Legs got froze. Feet froze. Boots wet." Each word a struggle, the string of comments became agonizing to witness. Josh shook Chase again, trying to keep him from falling back asleep. He then grabbed his friend's rifle case and slung it over his shoulder.

Uncle Jim grabbed Chase's wrists and began to pull him up. Chase swung his arm over Uncle Jim's shoulder and limped. His whole body was dead weight as Josh took the other arm over the shoulder.

Josh then glanced down at the bottom of the hill where the sled came to rest against a pine tree. Next to the sled, on its side, was a roped up buck. "You bagged a deer, Chase? Congrats!"

A weak smile crept across Chase's face, as a tinge of pink returned to his cheeks. "Thanks," he mumbled as his knees gave out for a moment. He attempted to turn his head to see where the deer landed.

"Do you want to bring it back to camp?"

"No. Leave it," Chase squeaked.

"C'mon. It's your first one. I'll bring it back."

"No, Josh. Let's go. Screw the deer," Uncle Jim broke in, huffing out each footstep.

"Want me to come back for it?"

"No. Leave it." Chase tried to yell.

Josh nodded, and shrugged, confused by his response. The three men trampled on as the snow tapered off. It was a welcome lull in the weather, although the wind continued to play with the snow piles like dunes in the desert. Crashing through the branches, Uncle Jim tried to keep Chase talking. Several times, Josh noticed Uncle Jim wincing in pain as Chase's body weight strained his weak leg.

"You'd make one tough soldier, kid. Shame you lost the deer, but we got to worry about the hospital first."

"Hospital?" Chase mumbled again, groggy. "Where's camp?"

"It's coming in sight now," Josh replied, pleading in silence that his father had prepared a place for Chase to warm up.

"How far have we gone? Miles? My feet feel like needles."

"Needles?" Josh asked. The raw wind buffeted their faces, and as they carried on Chase bobbed his head up on occasion as if to keep a fix on their location.

"Almost there," Uncle Jim reassured, puffing his way to the edge of the campsite. Josh and his uncle glanced at each other on occasion as Josh tried to ease all their worries with conversations of football.

"Neal!" Uncle Jim bellowed. "We need you!" All of a sudden, as if he was digging deeper within himself for one last burst of strength, Uncle Jim hoisted Chase completely off the ground the final twenty feet of the way.

At camp, Josh could see their food found a new home in a snow bank behind the cooking tent. Neal stood over a cooler, pouring steaming water from several pans into it. He then hauled the cooler back into the tent.

Neal then came to join the incoming wounded, relieving the stress off Uncle Jim's shoulders. "How bad is it?"

"Don't know until we get the boots off. Looks like he got bit on the ears. Got the water ready?"

"In the sleep tent. Got chicken soup going too." He turned to face Chase. "Can you feel your legs at all?"

"No. I mean sometimes. I stepped in some water." Chase arched his head back in pain and attempted to wiggle his fingers.

"Alright, we're going to get you warmed up and then I'm driving you into town to go to the hospital."

Uncle Jim did not argue this time. He hobbled into the cooking tent, as if his knee had sustained a hammer blow.

Josh and his father rested Chase on the edge of the foam mattress in the sleeping tent and immediately Josh undid his best friend's bootlaces. Neal scooped up a blanket, wrapping its heavy quilt around Chase's shoulders. Shivering out of control, Chase slid his mitts off, and extended his palms towards the propane heater. The steady hiss of the element and the crackling of the bonfire outside lulled him into a daydream of sorts.

Boot by boot, sock by sock, the damage became evident. Chase's feet had turned a faint pink, and almost white in patches. "You might make it out of this pretty well off," Neal observed. "You still have to go to the hospital, though. Here, put your feet in here."

Neal shoved the cooler in front of Chase's legs. Chase sighed in relief as he lowered his feet into the warm water bath. The sloshing water at his ankles soothed his feet at first, allowing him the chance to let the tension in his shoulders uncoil. He slipped off his stocking cap, wincing as his ears began to itch. Off came his jacket, but with it came an angry growl from his stomach.

Uncle Jim came into the tent next, cradling a steaming bowl of soup. He set it next to the cooler. "How's that feel?"

"Much better. Thank you for saving my life." Chase managed a smile before strange contortions overtook his face. He ground his teeth together and clawed at the edges of the mattress in a sudden fit of pain. His feet began their excruciating transformation back to normal, displaying shades of blue, red, and crimson as the blood flow returned. "What the…" He pulled his feet out and yelled. He lay back on the mattress for a minute, then sat up again and took a deep breath. He then slipped his feet back into the water.

"Try to keep them in. I know it's hard. I'm going to start the truck as soon as you get warmed up and eat," said Neal. He stepped out now and attended the bonfire. Uncle Jim left and joined him as Josh stepped out to survey the situation.

"Think he's going to make it?" Uncle Jim probed.

"Yeah. He'll be okay if we get out before the next squall hits. I want you guys to pack up as much as you can, but if the snow starts before you've got the tent pegs pulled, stay put. That's an order from your big brother." Neal said, gazing down to watch the flames. "As for what you did today, I couldn't have been prouder of you and Josh. But I don't think I'd ever do that again. Sending you out with your...you know..."

"Leg?" Uncle Jim replied.

"Yes."

"Give me a break. You sound worse than I used to. I'm over it. You know I would have put my life on the line for any of you. Anytime." Uncle Jim then reached over and slugged his brother's shoulder. "Start the truck. We've gotta get packing, too, bro. I don't want to go through this again."

"Me either."

Neal slugged his brother back.

"How deep is it on the road out?"

"Four to five inches. Both our trucks will make it."

"For now." Uncle Jim nodded and basked in the pulsing warmth of the fire. Neal walked over to his truck and cranked over the engine.

Josh returned inside. He swapped deer stories with Chase, but Josh conceded Chase's adventure trumped his own on numerous points. In between growls of agony, Chase peeked down at his feet, watching their normal color flush back. Chase then downed his soup.

Neal stepped in ten minutes later. "Ready to go?"

"Almost. Let me dress."

The others left the tent and when Chase finished dressing he called out to Neal and Josh.

They returned and scooped up two blankets as Chase put his jacket back on. He had already slipped his feet out of the water and toweled them off. He slipped on another pair of socks and then relied on two strong sets of shoulders to keep his feet off the ground.

After Chase became situated in the truck, Josh rapped on the passenger side window. "Are you sure you don't want me to get it?" He shouted, referring to the deer left in the woods.

"No. It is better left alone."

Chapter Twenty-Two

Neal and Chase rode out away from the campsite down the dirt road that ran to the nearest highway. The first four miles proved difficult, even with Neal's truck locked into four-wheel drive. Chase sat upright, constantly readjusting the layers of blankets covering him from neck to foot. He still had the shivers, although the spells grew further apart in frequency. The soup doubled his energy level, although a long nap still felt necessary.

The truck bounded and bounced through the hills and pits of the road and the truck fought to avoid getting stuck every half mile or so. Neal clicked on the radio to hear weather reports warning people to avoid travel if possible, which they both knew was impossible. "How are your feet doing?" He asked, looking down as if he could see through the socks and blankets.

"Good. A bit numb, but better."

Neal nodded and poked at the radio buttons. Another round of snow would hit tonight the radio said, and Chase hoped Uncle Jim and Josh broke camp before nightfall.

Chase watched as stray snowflakes careened into the headlights. The truck seemed to travel like a spaceship from the movies, journeying through time and bending all the rules of physics as stars barreled by. He gazed straight ahead as the truck finally came to a portion of the road with fresh tire tracks.

"Oh, by the way. If Josh talks about making a change in his life…" Chase thought for a moment. "Go easy on him."

Neal turned to Chase in silence. With a concerned and confused look, he replied, "I will." Neal hit the wash button, spewing the windshield with blue mist.

"By the way, what kind of change are we talking about?" He continued after a moment.

"He'll tell you on his own time." Chase sighed and knew sensed a collision of ideas was coming between Josh and his father, possibly before Christmas.

Ten minutes passed before the truck made it up onto the highway. Chase marveled at the wrath of the storm—trees, signs, power lines— all coated with the same sense of identity, the same sense of beauty, the same sense of burden. Even the passing sanding trucks looked as if they dumped out cinnamon and sugar on the ribbon of road before him.

Chase laughed.

"What's so funny?" Neal asked, switching off the radio.

"I should have had Josh go back and get that deer. Then I could have had the head mounted."

"It's a shame, I agree. But we can go back for it later or maybe even tomorrow."

Neal pointed to a hospital sign on the road. "There is something I don't understand, though. If you knew it was beginning to snow as hard as it was, why didn't you give up the chase?"

"Because once you get a hold of a dream like that, it's hard to let go."

"You're lucky you didn't lose your life out there today."

Chase nodded, then looked happily out the window. In many ways he figured, he was just beginning to get it back.

Chapter Twenty-Three

The house was dark and crowded until the floor lamp came to life. Karen turned on the radio to listen to the top stories of the afternoon, which included the snowstorm and reports of hunting accidents. After disrobing her jacket, she squatted down onto the sofa and hunched over to listen.

Three accidents had been reported so far, all related to hunters and all related to stray bullets. Two men had been shot, both in their thirties, both the northwest corner of the state. One died of a slug wound in his chest, while the other man was hospitalized with a leg wound.

The third incident involved a thirteen-year old boy, who was shot in the arm while hunting with a party in the fields of the southern part of the state. Although the accidents caused her to shudder beneath her blanket, it appeared Chase was safe, if only for the moment. She remained fixated on the speaker until a commercial came on, at which point she sprang up to make a telephone call.

In the kitchen the answering machine remained empty, although every machine she ever owned in her lifetime proved faulty in one manner or another. She picked up the receiver.

Karen rang Neal's house in hopes that his wife would answer, but no reply came. After leaving a message of her own, she hung up and then dialed her mother in Spokane.

"Mom? It's Karen."

"Hi, long time no hear from you. What's new?" Came a surprised voice from the other end.

"Not much. Chase went hunting this weekend with Josh and Josh's dad and Uncle, and now I am worried that something might have happened to him."

"Like what?"

"Well, I was at the mall this afternoon and a strange feeling came over me—kind of like the time Chase fell off his bicycle and broke his arm. And then I came home and turned on the radio and they said there had been a blizzard up where they are hunting."

"And you think he was hurt?"

Karen played with the phone cord, winding and unwinding the knots along its length.

"I'm not sure. I watched the news and there have been three hunting accidents already. But none of them were close to where they went. There haven't been any messages on my machine either."

"There's no way you can get a hold of him is there?"

"No." Karen stared out the window at the snow, which was being driven in harsh gusts. "It's snowing here, now, too."

"You say he went with Neal? Well, I'm sure they are fine," her mother soothed. "Neal is good about the weather. He's been through enough and I'm sure he wouldn't let anything happen to Chase."

"Think so?"

"Dear, it's like my mother said to me growing up. She said: Dear, you're never given more than you can handle."

"Meaning what?"

"Meaning you should have faith, dear. They'll make it through."

"But what if their truck gets stuck? Or if they get snowed in?"

"Karen, you're thinking too much. Find something to do and quit worrying."

"I'll try."

"Try harder."

"Thanks, Mom."

Karen then let her go, although she felt like apologizing for bringing her mother into this. She could not detect the slightest crackle in her mother's voice, which was a sure sign of unspoken concern. She then looked down at the kitchen table, and stared at the page that was open in her Bible. Her eyes drifted to Philippians 4:6: *"Be careful for nothing; but in every thing by prayer and supplication with thanksgiving let your requests be made known unto God."*

She then said a quick prayer for her son's safety. A moment later, another thought struck her. She looked up some passages on forgiveness and suddenly realized what she needed to tell Chase the next time she spoke to him.

Returning to the living room, she eyed the emptied easel and the stash of paints in waiting. The urge to create left her now in anticipation of word from up north. Any comfort would do—a knock at the door, a phone call or even her son alive and safe on her doorstep. The dream she dashed for only hours ago seemed a worthless race now in the face of all that really mattered to her.

She switched off the radio in exchange for the glow of the television, letting the remote control tumble onto the coffee table. Although no news reports were on now in the heart of the afternoon, she did appreciate the company of chatter. Then she returned to the kitchen to appreciate the contents of the refrigerator.

Chapter Twenty-Four

Neal pulled into the Virginia Hospital parking lot and helped Chase unbuckle his seat belt. Bundled in blankets, Chase hobbled his way with Neal's help through the automated sliding glass doors of the emergency entrance.

Chase still could not believe his second trip hunting ended up this way. Sure, there had been a moment of pride and glory when his marksmanship earned him a trophy buck. Now all he was going to have to show for it, however, were bandaged feet and ears, and this thought saddened him now.

The nurse at the reception desk looked up to greet them. Chase slipped his arm off of Neal's shoulder and dropped into a chair next to the desk. Both men sweated and panted, grateful.

"Need a wheelchair?" The nurse asked.

"That would be great, thanks," Neal replied.

An orderly dressed in blue garb soon appeared and pushed the wheelchair next to Chase. As he and Neal helped Chase into the seat, the nurse began asking names, getting details and taking notes.

"On the feet and both ears," she muttered to herself. "Okay. Take off your jacket and the blanket so I can get your blood pressure and take your temperature."

The nurse then uncoiled the blood pressure cuff and wrapped it around Chase's left arm. Although his head began to buzz now, he fought to relax. He read the name off her nametag: Amy.

"140 over 80." Amy pulled out a thermometer and took his temperature. His temperature was just below normal, which relieved him because it meant for the moment he dodged hypothermia.

"And how long do you think you were out?"

"Five minutes, maybe."

"You're lucky." She turned to glare at Neal. "You his father?"

"No, his friend's dad. We got there as fast as we could..."

88

"I'm sure you did. We'll get you taken care of." She stroked Chase's arm after pulling off the cuff. "Poor thing."

"Must be big news when a snow like this comes through," Neal laughed.

"Really. Nothing else going on up here. Glad I'm going back."

"Back where?"

"Back to Saint Paul. I used to live up here when I was little. Came back and I didn't realize how quiet it really was. Too quiet. Miss the sirens, believe it or not."

"Do you miss the crime, too?"

"No, no. Guess that's the good thing about it up here. I must seem like one strange nurse, huh?" She patted Chase on the arm again and smiled. Amy handed him his registration papers and directed him to the lobby.

"Need help with the chair?"

"No, no. We got it," Neal replied.

"Ok, well, Dr. Hale will be the one to see you next."

"Thanks. Good luck back home," Chase added.

Amy smiled and disappeared into a nearby hallway.

"Wonder why she moved back up in the middle of nowhere?"

"Probably tried to come back to something that wasn't there. She's probably a city girl now. Put her out in the open and she can't stand the silence." He turned to face Chase. "I should know, I married one."

Neal wheeled Chase over to the waiting lobby and there they stayed for twenty minutes until another nurse called for him. Neal helped him through another set of doors and down a mazework of corridors to a room. After the nurse entered some information into a computer, she left the room, followed by Neal.

A few minutes later, Dr. Hale arrived, whistling a tune that seemed to be of his own creation. Chase already sat at the edge of the padded and papered examination table, having stripped to his underwear and slipped on a hospital gown with enough gaps to make him shiver again.

Chase wanted to grab a nearby blanket, but instead waited as the doctor with the big bushy eyebrows and shiny cheeks examined his chart.

"I see. Hi there. I'm Dr. Hale. Hunting. Found face down in the snow. Hmmm," the doctor began. He appeared to be in his fifties and spoke with a gravelly German accent. "Were you hunting with a group or by yourself?"

"With a friend and his family. They put my feet in some warm water. They said they found me with facedown and laying on my rifle case."

"Yes, yes. Good. Well, not good, but we get these all the time. People fall through the ice, don't wear hats…says here you think you froze your ears and feet." He gazed over the clipboard, directing Chase to prop his feet onto the table. Chase obliged but squeezed the padding of the table when the doctor began poking and prodding at his toes.

"Looks like a bit of white here. Should heal on its own. Nothing blue, nothing black, that's good. As for your ears…" Dr. Hale tipped back his head and squinted through his bifocals.

"Ouch!" Chase yelped, irritated by the onslaught of burly fingers on his tender ears.

"The ears need salve and bandages. The nurse will fix you up." Dr. Hale smiled again, hoping to ease Chase's grief. "You'll be as good as new in two weeks." He laughed. "For that matter, so will I."

"Going on vacation?"

"No, no. Retiring. I'll be flying cross-country in my two-seater next week. As for you, young man, you'll be fine." The doctor then waved on the nurse and left the room.

"Ow. Thanks," Chase mumbled, feeling a blister building on his ear. The cold that took a bite out of his ears now began taking one out of his stamina. He grimaced again after the nurse arrived and began her own work.

At the merciful end of the ordeal, the nurse exited the room, leaving the door open. Neal returned to help Chase back into the wheelchair. "I know it seems cruel to ask, but are you feeling better now?"

"Actually, yes. Think the others are okay?"

"I'm not sure. I think Jimmy will get them out before dark. He said he'd call when he got out and made it to a pay phone. Speaking of that, I should call home in an hour and see if he left a message."

Chase detected a tinge of worry in Neal's voice, even a measure of guilt. He could sense Neal wanted to run back north in his truck, and Chase decided he wanted to also. That is, if Neal would let him.

"Think we should go back for them?"

Neal sighed. "I think they'll be okay." He turned to face Chase. "I think you should call your mom, though."

"I don't want to worry her."

"Believe me, she probably already is if she watches television or listens to the radio."

Chase reclined in his wheelchair and looked around the room. "Couldn't we get something to eat first?"

"Call."

"Fine. Gimme some quarters."

Chase wheeled over to a pay phone and methodically pumped the change into the coin slot. He dialed and waited only one ring before his mother answered.

"Hello?" Came an anxious gasp at the other end.

"Hi, Mom. It's Chase."

"Where the…are you?"

"Relax. I'm okay. I'm at a pay phone."

"A pay phone where?"

"In Virginia."

"Are you okay? Is everything alright?"

"Well, no. I'm at a hospital. I got frostbite in a couple places, but I'm bandaged and okay now. I'll be home soon." Chase peered over at Neal with a helpless gaze.

"I'm coming up there right now. What hospital again?"

Chase could hear his mother shuffling a piece of paper in the background. "Mom, you can't. Snow's coming again, and you'll get stuck. Stay home. Neal's driving me home right away."

"No, I'm coming. What's the address?"

"Stay, Mom. By the time you'd get here, we could be gone. If we don't go soon, we'll get stranded. Please, stay."

Karen grumbled. "Okay. But when you come home you're going to bed. Got it?"

"I suppose. Oh, and by the way, Mom. I got a deer."

"You did?" Warmth surged back into her voice.

"Yup. But I had to leave it behind, though."

"Are you sad now?"

He exhaled a deep breath. "Yes and no." Reaching into his jacket, which lay across his lap, he withdrew the tiny carving his mother sent

91

along with him. "I still have what really matters, I guess. So did you go to the sale?"

"Yes. And you'll never believe who I met there."

"Who?"

"Steve."

"Dating Steve?"

"Yes, and he's opened up an exhibit at the museum for locals like me."

Chase slouched back into his wheelchair, drumming his fingers on the armrest. "Where's the painting now?"

"I almost forgot. I left it in the backseat of the car."

"And he offered to put it in the show? For what?"

"For nothing. Aren't you happy?"

Chase sat in silence for a moment. "Seems like a generous offer. I'm happy for you. Truly."

"Thanks. Oh, and by the way…on the way back from the mall I picked up a pad of paper and envelopes for your letter writing."

Chase reflected on the pact he made to himself in the woods. He thought about bringing it up, but decided not to give breath to it and to keep it locked away in his heart.

"I appreciate that, Mom. But I don't think I'll be needing those things anymore."

There was a moment of silence that seemed to last a minute or more.

"Chase…"

"Yeah, Mom?"

There was another moment of silence.

"Can I let you in on something?"

"Sure."

"Do you know what I did a few years after your father and I broke up?"

"No. I mean, not really."

"I forgave him."

He took in a deep breath and sighed.

"I'm not going to tell you what to do about this, but I hope you come to a point where you can do the same. And then when you've done that, forgive yourself."

Chase sat silent for a few more seconds. "You know, you're probably right."

Chapter Twenty-Five

After Neal and Chase ate downstairs in the hospital cafeteria, Neal wandered over to a pay phone himself. When the connection went through he smiled over at Chase. "Hi, Kate? It's Neal. No, no, we're okay. Had a bit of trouble. Yes, we're okay now. Did Jimmy call?"

Neal stood silent, and all Chase could hear was chatter through the receiver. A broad smile exploded across Neal's face and he nodded at Chase. "I didn't think he was that fast. Must have thrown the stuff in and ran."

"What? We're okay. Stopped in town for a bite to eat."

More chatter.

"Josh went back for it, huh?"

Chase figured Neal was referring to the buck he lost in the woods.

"Okay. Listen, I'll explain more when we get home." Neal winked to Chase and leaned against the wall. "Yes. Yes. He's fine now. Boy's got a lot of luck on his side or someone's watching over him, that's for sure."

Chase slid on his jacket, sleeve by delicate sleeve, and began to button it. The cafeteria remained empty, save for a pair of surgical orderlies and a female doctor poring over a newspaper and her spaghetti.

Neal glanced back at Chase, smiling. "Yes. The man's going to make out just fine in this world."

Chase closed his eyes for a moment and daydreamt of the future design of his architectural firm.

About the Author

Michael Galloway is an outdoors enthusiast whose interests include camping, fishing, hiking, writing, and technology. He has a degree in Journalism, and has been writing software in one language or another for over forty years. He currently lives in Minnesota with his family.

* * *

Also by Michael Galloway

Theft at the Speed of Light
Horizons
Gathering the Wind
Corridors
Fractal Standard Time
Ionotatron
Chronopticus Rising
The Chronopticus Chronicles
Race the Sky
The Hammer of Amalynth
Windows Out
The Fire and the Anvil
Gathering the Artists
Gathering the Swarm
Gathering the Hours
Flyover Country

www.ingramcontent.com/pod-product-compliance
Lightning Source LLC
Chambersburg PA
CBHW020633130626
46552CB00003B/1211